dog days

and other stories

Introduction by Joseph O'Connor

Edited by Clem Cairns

Fish Publishing
Durrus, Bantry, Co. Cork
Ireland

Published in Ireland by
Fish Publishing, 1997
Durrus, Bantry, West Cork

This book is published with the assistance of

The Arts Council
An Chomhairle Ealaíon

Supported by the
ARTS
COUNCIL

of Northern Ireland

ISBN 0 9523522 1 4
A catalogue record of this book is available from the British Library

Cover Painting, 'New Beginnings 2', by Amanda Addison.

Proof reading by Kelly-Hoffman, Ahakista, Bantry, Co. Cork.

This book is for
Sam, Autumn, Liam and Holly

Contents

Editor's Note

I edited this book on dry land. Read the stories there too. A pleasant change from the last time when much of the work for *The Stranger and Other Stories* was done on a bobbing trawler south west of the Fastnet Rock. Diesel, dampness, and of course, fish!

There were over 1,000 stories this time, and the overall standard was higher. Congratulations, therefore, to the fourteen authors who made it into this book, and in particular to Karl Iagnemma from Boston who won the first prize of £1,000 for his story *Dog Days.*

Joseph O'Connor, Jennifer Johnston, and Emma Donoghue were the final judges. Thanks to them for their interest, time and wisdom.

Three of last year's winners have since had books of their own published - Molly McCloskey's *Solomon's Seal,* Eamonn Sweeney's *Waiting For The Healer,* and Suzanne Power's *Being You.* All are working on their next book.

Francis Humphries, Clodagh Simmonds, and Sarah Cairns helped with the reading, and Diane Martin achieved wonders in administration.

In the USA John and Maggie Sweeney looked after the e mails, web pages, letters - and in the UK Sue and Gerald Hart did the business, many thanks!

The cover painting, *New Beginnings 2,* by Amanda Addison won a competition for the painting to feature on the cover of this book. Enjoy the £500 prize Amanda and thank you William Crozier for judging the art work. Details of the '98 cover competition are available from Fish Publishing.

Tommy and Yvonne Ungerer donated the £1,000 for the

short story prize. Credit and thanks is due to them for this and their on-going support for the arts.

The Fish Short Story Prize is an annual event. The judges this year are Germaine Greer, Eamonn Sweeney, and Pat Boran. The closing date is 30th November. The full details are at the back of this book. Your story could be in the next anthology. Get writing!

Introduction

What kind of strange creature is a short story writer? I must confess that I don't know. A high priest or priest of art? A wounded soul who can't understand the real world and thus feels a need to re-invent it? A moralist? A spinner of yarns? An entertainer? A prophet? Probably all of these things. Possibly none.

The single fact I can be sure about is this: writers are watchers. The one and only thing they have in common is an ability to look at the everyday world and be knocked out by it. Stopped in their tracks. Startled. Gobsmacked.

My favourite short story writer, Raymond Carver, has this to say:

Writers don't need tricks or gimmicks, or even necessarily need to be the smartest fellows on the block. At the risk of appearing foolish, a writer sometimes needs to be able to just stand and gape at this or that thing - a sunset, or an old shoe - in absolute and simple amazement.

Another writer I love, Flannery O'Connor, put it even more strongly:

There is a certain grain of stupidity that the writer of fiction can hardly do without, and this is the quality of having to stare, of not getting the point at once.

There is only one trait that writers have in common and that's it. They watch for the extraordinary magic that lies in the everyday. A writer is always quietly looking and thinking. Not willing inspiration but just being open to the world. This quiet looking and thinking is the imagination. It's letting in ideas. It's trying, I suppose, to make some sense of things.

In that sense, it is important for a writer to be always writing.

Even when you're not actually sitting with a pen in your hand. You don't take days off. You don't go on holiday from writing. Sometimes you don't even go to sleep. If you're serious about writing - as the people whose fine work is represented here most definitely are - then you're a writer twenty-four hours a day, in the office, in school, doing the dishes and in your dreams.

Writers have their eyes open. They keep them open all the time.

Ezra Pound said 'fundamental accuracy of statement is the *one* morality of writing'. Naming things, calling things what they really are. This is all that writers can do in an age where language has become debased and sterile. That is what the writers in this book do, time and again, with style and conviction and confidence.

Most of them are spare time writers, in the sense that they do other things to make money. But you'd never guess that from their work. James Thurber was a full-time writer. His use of his spare time is interesting:

I never quite know when I'm not writing. Sometimes my wife comes up to me at a party and says, 'Dammit, Thurber, stop writing'. She usually catches me in the middle of a paragraph. Or my daughter will look up from the dinner table and ask, Is he sick? 'No', my wife says, 'he's writing something'.

That we all do what Thurber did is important, if we want to be more than dilettantes, if we want to achieve the admirably high standards of the work represented in this collection. Writing is not typing. Writing is, first of all, a way of looking at the world, naming it precisely, making sense of it or celebrating its nonsense.

The short story is one of the greatest, most challenging, most infuriating forms of literature. They look so easy! That's the thing about really good short stories like these. They don't read like they were written. They read like they simply grew on the page. When we read the work of a short story maestro like Joyce or Frank O'Connor or Richard Ford or Alice Monroe or Mary Lavin, we think *yes,* there is just a rightness about that sentence, that image, that line of speech. But anyone who has ever tried to write a short story will know just how tough it is to hit that reverberating note, to say something - anything at all - worthwhile about the human condition in five thousand words or less. It's hard.

A short story is a glance at the miraculous. Joyce used a religious word. He called his stories 'epiphanies'. A good short story is almost always about a moment of profound realisation. Or a hint of that. A quiet bomb. There is a record by the American singer Tori Amos called *Little Earthquakes.* That's a good metaphor for a short story. Often, a good short story will be a little earthquake.

It is a form that has all the power of the novel - some would say more - but none of the self-importance. A deftly imagined and carefully written short story like Karl lagnemma's *Dog Days,* or Frank O'Donovan's *Johnny Mok's Universe,* or Anne O'Carroll's *Flame,* by concentrating on the particular, can say a whole lot about the universal.

So let us get idealistic for a second or two. V.S. Pritchett's description of a short story is 'something glimpsed from the corner of the eye, in passing'. And our task as short story writers is to grab that moment with both hands and invest it with all of the power and humanity and sympathy we can. To develop our skill at language and characterisation and structure and dialogue - our fundamental accuracy - for one reason. To tell the truth. That's what all the hard work comes down to in the end.

If we forget that, we forget everything.

Joseph O'Connor
Dublin, 1997

v

Karl Iagnemma

Winner of the 1996/97 Fish Short Story Prize

I grew up in Detroit, but now live in Boston and study mechanical engineering at MIT, where I spend most of my time dreaming about the day when I'll receive my PhD. and can give up engineering for good. Before MIT I spent a year at Trinity College Dublin, and am still recovering. When I'm not studying or writing, I can be found wandering around Boston, impersonating a normal human being.

Dog Days

Karl Iagnemma

A woman named Sandy was teaching us how to breathe. 'Think of pools of deep water,' she said. She inhaled deeply, lifting her arms above her head, then exhaled. 'Synchronise your breathing with your child's. Mothers, *listen* to your bodies.' Sandy smiled peacefully. 'Focus on the rhythm of your breathing. Place everything else aside.'

It was the third week, and we still didn't have it right. Christina was lying in my lap on the floor, sweating. She was in her seventh month, and enormous. 'I'm so goddamn *hot*,' she hissed. 'I'm burning up.'

Sandy came over to check on us. She was a heavy woman who wore tie-dye and sandals, and used words like *energy* and *rhythm* and *aura*. Christina hated her. 'Our young couple is doing wonderfully,' Sandy announced, smiling. She whispered, 'You both look so happy.'

I was nineteen years old, Christina was twenty. We were trying to do it right: birth classes, showers, Doctor Spock. We'd turned the spare room into a baby room, with fuzzy bear wall paper, a crib full of soft, jingly toys, a pink and yellow mobile. The room once held my dart board, and sometimes I'd stumble in late at night and turn on the light, and when those colours hit me I'd remember who I was.

During the rest period we sat in the lobby of the clinic, trying to cool down, and Christina started naming off more things to buy for the baby room, more ideas for a middle name, and then she said, 'I've been thinking that we should get rid of Uno before the baby comes.'

Uno was my dog, a yellow Lab. A big dog, but gentle as a rabbit.

She went on: 'The more I think about it, the more I don't like the idea of having a dog around a baby. Have you noticed how sometimes he just *looks* at you? I don't know.' She rested her hands on her swollen belly. 'I've heard about too many accidents. And non-accidents.'

I chuckled. 'You're thinking of cats. They sit on the kids' chests so they can't breathe. And it's no accident - cats do that on purpose. They're jealous animals.'

'Cooper,' she said, 'I'm serious. This is something I'm asking you to do.' She took my hand. 'I'm thinking about our son, that's all. I worry about him so much.'

Sandy announced that break time was over. We went back in. Christina settled herself carefully in my lap and inhaled, and I squeezed her hand like I was supposed to.

'Pretend that you're blowing out a candle,' Sandy advised.

I whispered, 'I grew up with a dog. A German Shepherd named Armstrong.'

'I know,' she puffed.

'The ones you have to worry about are Pit Bulls and Rottweilers.'

She turned back halfway toward me. 'I don't want to argue, honey. I'm so sick of fighting.'

I whispered, 'When my father would go out drinking, he'd never pay for a sitter: he'd let the dog watch my sister and me. That's the truth.'

Now she sat up, turned and stared at me, incredulous. 'My

2

God, Cooper,' she said. She shook her head. 'I knew your father was an asshole, but Jesus. That's the most irresponsible thing I've ever heard.' She leaned her head back against my chest, and inhaled.

Last May, during an argument over the television, Christina threw a heavy glass ashtray at me and hit me in the right temple. While a young doctor gave me three quick stitches in emergency, Christina filled out the forms. The doctor asked me what had happened; I told him I fell off a ladder.

When we got to the car, Christina cried hysterically. 'I know, I know. I'm terrible.' She sobbed. 'I'm so bad. I'm so bad.' She hugged me tight and buried her wet face in my neck, then she kissed my bandage gently. I was so bruised, her lips felt like sledgehammers.

I told her, 'It's okay. I love you. I understand.' I felt heroic, as though I'd done something deserving praise. That night she pressed her naked body close against me and whispered *I want to be nice to you*. I told her, *You can't. My head hurts too much.*

Around that time, I began going out on Wednesday nights with three guys from work to a bar called Sallie Mae's, where I'd get utterly shitfaced, pass out, and end up being carried like a child to my door by a spot-welder named Kenny. At Sally Mae's, we'd sit at the bar and drink boilermakers, throw darts, and try to talk to the bony, desperate women who'd sit at the other end of the bar and fix their lipstick and pretend to ignore us.

One night a tall, average-looking woman kissed me, hard and long, while my friends stared into their beers. And there's this - I kissed her back. I was drunk, but I was thinking about my wife and her belly, how she reminded me of a textbook picture of a snake that had eaten something impossibly big. When we finished, I told the woman that in four months I would be a father. She said *Well isn't that sweet?* and went back to her corner of the bar.

The next week our doctor, Doctor Fang, rubbed a clear jelly on

Christina's stomach, then waved a magic wand, and - presto! - a fuzzy blob, our child, squirmed and kicked on the screen in front of us. Christina started to cry, and I suddenly had a tremendous feeling of speed, like I was driving my Mustang faster and faster down a steep hill. I had to sit down. Doctor Fang smiled proudly, although she'd done this a thousand times. 'You have a boy,' she told us. 'A son.'

The next Sunday at birth class, I made Christina cry. There was a time when we would drive down Van Dyke past the orchards, turn down one of the rutted, empty side-roads, and climb into the back seat of the Mustang, giggling. This was not so long ago - we were married - but our apartment couldn't hold us. Even the vacant fields seemed pitifully small.

Now, I picked on her. I asked her about her sister Suzanne, the shoplifter, or I talked about money. Today I'd been telling her about the day I'd found Uno, a frozen December Monday: he'd been a small, cold lump huddled underneath my father's truck, and I'd held him inside my jacket to warm him up. I knew exactly what to say.

The other couples in the class looked away, but Sandy came over and asked, 'Is there anything I can do?' Her wide, peaceful face was creased with worry.

'Please go away,' Christina said, through her tears. 'Please.'

The dog had become an issue. Christina wanted me to find it a new home; I wanted it to stay. The tough thing was, I could see her point - a big dog and a small child - and I also knew she wouldn't back down.

On the way home I stopped at the Dairy Queen drive-thru. 'Peanut buster parfait? Or a blizzard?'

She gave a moist sigh. 'This is what we do. Fight and eat ice cream. Fight and have sex. It's pathetic.'

I said, 'Which?'

'Blizzard.'

We sat in the parking lot, eating.

4

'I wish you weren't so nervous,' Christina said. 'You don't make things much easier.'

'I'm not that nervous.'

'You forget that I'm here, too. You act like you're going through this all by yourself. Selfish, is what you're being.'

'What do I do? I take drives at night. And that means I'm selfish?'

Christina sighed.

She was, in fact, exactly right. She was pregnant - I had no idea what that meant. At night I would press my ear against her stomach, expecting muffled aquatic sounds, like those from a fish tank. I don't know what I hoped to hear - secret whispers from my unborn son, maybe a little advice. In the morning, after her shower, I would see her naked, and my stomach would lift, fluttering like a trapped bird.

'Why am I ready for this and you aren't?' she wondered. 'What's happening here?'

On Van Dyke, a long firetruck rushed by, sirens howling. Another, smaller truck followed. They were headed north, where a thin grey column of smoke was rising and spreading out.

'Look,' I said. 'Some punks set the high school on fire again.'

She said, 'Good.'

Our baby was conceived on January sixth. Sometimes I wished I could rewind that day to its beginning: not get out of bed, or drive as far as my car would take me, or pretend I was someone completely different.

Afterwards, Christina had said, 'I feel you inside me, honey. I feel it.' I rolled off her. 'Jesus Christ.'

'Hug me.'

'Christina - my God - Christina.'

'I know. Hug me. I love you. You're inside me right now.'

Christina told me she was pregnant in the middle of an argument. She threw the words at me. We'd been married six months, living in a too-small apartment in Utica and drinking most nights, bitching about the people above us, buying stupid, expensive furniture that we immediately hated. It was clear that we annoyed each other. Christina couldn't understand my snoring, or my dirty dishes in the bedroom, or how I could walk naked through the apartment after a shower, dripping - she thought I did these things specifically to agitate her.

We decided to buy a house, and although we had almost no money, we found a small 1950's one-story in Romeo, two small bedrooms and a kitchen with warped linoleum and rotten cabinets. I drywalled the family room, re-tiled the bathroom and installed storm windows. The wiring was old, not close to code, and the front lawn needed sod. My neighbour, a fat, older man named Gene, would tell me, 'I don't know why you bother - that resale isn't going anywhere but down. Way out here? Come on.'

In Romeo, you sit in your back yard on spring nights, drinking Busch and watching the Tigers as the night fades in. Mosquitoes are a problem, but for them we have jumbo-sized bug zappers, powerful globes that cast a flat, dusty light on everything. The winey apple smell from the orchards drifts in on the breeze.

Those first months, Christina was tired, and she had to pee, but otherwise she was calm. The baby was a slight, smooth crest under her knee-length T-shirt. I'd rub her shoulders and we'd talk about the future, as if things were only improving, or at least holding steady. Arguments, if they appeared, were mild.

'What are the chances?' she'd ask me.

'Pretty good. Ray is retiring at the end of the year, and there's no one else.'

'And what do we do? You promised, don't forget.'

'I know. The Monte Carlo.'

'Oh,' she sighed. 'I want leather seats. Soft black leather.'

We'd turn off the TV, and the quiet was amazing: crickets, a far-off radio, the occasional rush of a passing truck. If I closed my eyes it was like we were off in deep space, floating.

6

The Sunday of our final birth class - the first day of Christina's eighth month - I drove over to my foreman's house. Jerry lives in Milford on three acres with woods and a stream and an old smokehouse that local kids claimed was haunted. Most Sundays I stopped over and turned Uno loose - it was paradise for him - and Jerry and I would drink a few Millers on the front porch, with the TV inside tuned to the baseball game.

Jerry was in his garage when we pulled up. 'Good timing,' he said. 'I've got a project for us.' I freed Uno; he pawed Jerry briefly, then ambled toward the woods.

Jerry was in his thirties, which might account for his tendency to give me advice. Once, at Sallie Mae's, he'd said, 'I'm looking out for you.' He'd put his arm around my shoulder. 'You're my boy, Cooper. You're like my kid.' He was drunk.

I said, 'Quit it. I hated my father.'

'You're my kid,' he insisted.

Now, from the back of the garage, Jerry called, 'We're knocking down the smokehouse.' He heaved a sledgehammer onto the lawn.

'I thought you liked the smokehouse.'

'Shithead kids,' he said. He emerged with a crowbar and another sledgehammer, red-faced. 'One of them cut their hand on a nail, fucking around in there. His mother threatened to sue. So, screw it.'

The smokehouse was a low, windowless building, the size of a luxury outhouse. Inside, the rich hickory smell was strong, although it hadn't been used in years.

'This thing is probably sixty years old,' Jerry said, peering through the low doorway. 'So much for history.' He crouched in a stance like a baseball player, then slammed his hammer against the side of the building. A large chunk of wood cracked inward.

I hit a cross-beam with my first swing; the wood split only slightly, and the hammer shivered like a swarm of bees. Jerry

7

chuckled. 'There. And there,' he said, pointing. 'Not there.'

We worked quickly, ripping gaping chunks from the old building. It was a cloudless ninety degrees. Jerry took off his shirt, and the thick hair on his back was matted and swirled, like crop patterns. 'Somebody gave a shit when they built this,' he rasped. 'Solid.'

After a half hour, we had most of it knocked down; the roof was crumpled inside, and only one wall was still standing. My hands were sweaty and sore. I suggested a break, but Jerry wanted to finish up before the Tigers started, at three.

I said, 'They should make people pass an asshole test before they can have kids. What do you think?'

'Agreed,' Jerry said. He switched to the crowbar, pried a plank away from the corner post.

'Then again, if that had been around when my folks got married, I wouldn't be here. My old man was certifiable.'

He nodded. 'The question is, would you pass that test yourself? That's the real question.' He chuckled.

'You're right,' I said. 'I don't know the answer to that one.'

Jerry said, 'I was your age when I got married. That's why I'm divorced.' He lifted the hammer to his shoulder. The veins on his forearms stood out like snakes. 'No. That's not what I mean.'

I said, 'I know what you mean. It's okay.'

Jerry sighed thoughtfully. I prepared for one of his sweeping statements. It was: 'That's life. They say you have a choice in things, but you don't. You just plain don't.' He jerked his head toward the ruined shed. 'Look at the way this thing was made. Beautiful.' He shook his head. Then he shrugged the hammer off his shoulder, slammed it against the broken timbers.

I said, 'Christina's been bugging me to get rid of Uno when the baby comes.'

'So?'

'So it's a big deal, I guess.'

Jerry frowned. 'Personally, I could never understand getting too close to an animal. Dog's a dog. If it dies, you buy a new one. Besides, this is your kid we're talking about, Cooper.'

I know,' I said. 'I'm going to do it.'

Jerry nodded. 'Good.' He delivered another loud *whack* to the splintered planks. 'Settle down. Do the right thing. Quit acting like a goddamn kid.'

I nodded. 'Why didn't you and Angela ever have kids?'

Jerry straightened up. He wiped his face carefully. 'It didn't work, is all. I couldn't deliver. My fault.'

'You saw doctors? They told you for sure?'

'Some things you just know.' He shrugged. 'Maybe I failed the asshole test.'

We were drinking beer on Jerry's porch. The timbers from the smokehouse were piled in the bed of his Ram. He was in full sermon mode.

'The burning house test,' he intoned.

'Fine. What is it?'

'It's simple.' He frowned at his beer can, then took a long drink. 'You're driving home from work one night. It's late. It's midnight. Let's say you worked overtime, and then you stopped at Wendy's for a burger. Anyway, you're turning into your subdivision when you hear this explosion, and suddenly the house on your right is on fire. Smoke pouring out the windows. So you stop, of course, and you get out of your truck, but no one else is around, and no one's come out of the house. And you know these people, you know they've got a kid.'

'How old?'

'Say, two years old. A baby. Would you go in and save that child? That's the only question here.'

I sipped my beer. Uno's bark echoed from somewhere in the direction of the stream, and another, deeper bark echoed back. 'I would,' I said. 'I'd go in after the kid, sure.'

Jerry nodded slowly. 'That's the wrong answer. Have you ever heard of 911? That's a teenager's answer.'

'I'm a teenager,' I said.

'So quit acting like one.' He frowned earnestly at me. 'Get your head on straight, Cooper. Goddamn.'

On the way home from Jerry's, I stopped at Meijer's for a frozen pizza and a small bouquet of daisies. Christina had fallen asleep at the kitchen table, her head resting on a crocheted pot holder. I woke her by whispering her name over and over. We ate pizza standing in the kitchen, a livid waffle pattern imprinted on my wife's right cheek.

'So what's the timetable for the dog?'

As if on cue, Uno trotted into the kitchen, toenails clicking. He sniffed after the pizza.

'Soon,' I said.

She nodded. 'What do you think of Henry? Too old-fashioned?'

'I like it.'

She rested her hands on her stomach. She was wearing a purple night-dress with small buttons and lace at the collar, a gift from her grandmother. She looked down at herself. 'Are you scared of me?' she asked.

I shook my head.

'Sometimes I can't believe it when I get out of the shower. I look in the mirror, and I get so nervous.' She smiled. 'I feel amazing. It's my *body*. I wish I could explain it.'

I put my hand on her stomach and held it there.

She said, 'Be nice to me tonight.' It was our code language.

I said, 'Anything you want, honey.'

The summer lingered, our tomato plants wrinkled and died, and Christina grew larger. Her moods were unpredictable. 'I love you,' she told me, in the morning before work. 'I love the way you drink coffee. You have a great ass. Kiss me.'

The assembly line didn't stop. I stitched ten thousand car seats or more. Uno chased tired cats and slept in his house by the shed, thirsty and ignorant. Christina nudged me, she'd ask, 'When?' or else she'd stare at him angrily, mumbling.

And then on a sweltering Tuesday, I came home from work to find Christina in the back yard, prying at the roof of Uno's house with a claw hammer. She'd already dislodged three of the dull white boards. Uno was stretched out a few feet away, his chin resting comfortably on his crossed paws, watching.

'What's going on?'

'Nothing,' she gasped. 'I thought, you know, I'd do this now. Get it over with.' Her big T-shirt was stretched over her shoulders and belly, stained with dark sweat circles. Her fine brown hair clung to her forehead and cheeks in whorls.

'You shouldn't be doing this,' I said, resting my hand on her forearm. 'It isn't good for you.'

She shrugged. 'Someone has to do it. I don't see anyone else doing it.' She wedged the hammer underneath the next plank, and wrenched it downward.

'Come on,' I said, 'it's way too hot. Come inside.'

She shook her head, her lips pursed. 'It won't get done, Cooper.'

'I'll do it,' I shouted. 'Jesus!'

Christina looked down at her grass-stained sneakers. 'I had a dream about that dog last night. That *fucker*. And I woke up and you were already gone to work.' She looked at me, squinting against the sun. 'You have a cold heart,' she said, nodding to herself. 'I'm going to take a shower.' She handed me the hammer, and waddled slowly toward the house.

I took off my shirt. Next door, Gene was in his back yard, watering his tomato plants with a hose. He watched me work, shaking his head.

'Mind your own business, Gene,' I called. 'We're doing just fine here.'

Gene said, 'Cooper -'

I raised my hand. 'Nothing else,' I said. 'Not another word.'

That Wednesday at Sallie Mae's, Rich said, 'She's tearing your balls off. Keep the dog.'

'Keep it,' Kenny said. 'Jesus, don't get rid of Uno. That's a great mutt.'

'He's not a mutt,' I said. 'He's a golden Lab. Pure-bred, I think.'

'Whatever,' Kenny said. 'Keep it.'

Sallie Mae's was nearly empty. It was the four of us sitting at the bar, and three couples at corner tables. The jukebox wasn't even playing.

Rich said, 'I had a little bulldog when I was a kid, named Rufus. Goddamn dog, he had one ear torn off in a fight, these big scars on his neck. He wouldn't let anyone feed him - he'd get stiff and bark like hell, and he did this drooling thing that scared my mother.' He shook his head. 'Then one night our neighbour wings him with a deer rifle - a thirty-thirty, I think - and takes his foreleg *clean off*. Told us he was tired of Rufus pissing on his rose bushes.'

'Rich,' Kenny said, 'what's your point?'

'My point is - keep the dog. That's all I'm saying.'

I said, 'Sure, guys: keep the dog and get rid of Christina. No problem.'

Kenny shrugged. 'Hey. No one's saying that.'

Later, in the john, Jerry said, 'Cooper, you got bigger things to think about than that dog. Do you know how much work a kid is? I don't know what it is with you.'

I said, 'I know. I know.'

'If I were in your shoes, I'd -'

'What?'

He shook his head. 'Nothing.'

That night, when I closed the bedroom door, Christina woke up. 'What time is it?' she slurred.

'Three,' I slurred back.

She didn't say anything, like she'd fallen back asleep. I stripped off my clothes and climbed under the sheets, and then she spoke again, completely awake. She asked me, 'What's up, honey?'

I said, 'You're tearing my balls off.'

'What?'

'Nothing.' I rolled over to escape the spinning room. 'I'm drunk.'

'I know. God, you smell like a bum.'

'I feel like a bum.'

She shifted close to me. 'I know how you feel about Uno, but this doesn't have to be so big, does it? I'm not trying to tear your balls off, or anything like that. I'm thinking about our little boy - that's all.'

I didn't say anything.

'This doesn't have to be so... male.'

'I don't know what you mean.'

'I mean, this isn't about Uno, is it?' She squeezed against me. 'This is the most natural thing. It's the most beautiful, natural thing. You don't need to be anxious.'

'I know. I know that.'

'Good.'

I closed my eyes. The room was slowing down. I said, 'Fine, okay. I'll get rid of the dog.'

She sighed. She touched my hair softly. 'We'll find him a good home.'

'Christina', I said, 'I will work my whole life for you.'

'That's sweet,' she said. 'Go to sleep.'

'Okay,' I said. 'Okay. I'm asleep.'

That weekend I finished our son's crib. The baby room was light blue, traditional, and already stocked with a year's worth of toys. We'd been given most of the things at an enormous baby shower, but I'd built the crib by hand out of maple. It had taken me four Saturdays, but it was a beautiful piece of work.

First I'd turned thirty identical coke-bottle shaped side-bars on Jerry's lathe. I'd sanded each of them so smooth that if you closed your eyes you'd swear they were glass. The joints in the frame were mortise-and-tenon, no shortcuts, and the tiny headboard was covered with carved scrollwork. I'd matched the grain of each piece perfectly, so that when you looked at it, the lines formed a neat, tight box, as though it could never be anything except a crib. Christina cried when she saw it.

While I worked on the crib I thought about names. I liked the name Lance, but was that a full name? And if not, what was the long version - Lancelot? That wouldn't work.

I wanted a son named Michael. Mike. It was a first name people would use; I didn't want my son to have a name like Cooper. My own first name was, of course, one of my father's ideas. It's a source of moderate embarrassment for me. Christina uses it only when she's very angry, or drunk, or teasing in a half-mean way.

One night I asked her what she thought of Michael, and she said she thought it was fine, just fine.

On the last Saturday in August I leashed Uno and dumped him in the passenger's seat of the Mustang. I drove out to Armada, where everything smelled of ripe, rotting apples, and pulled off the road and let Uno go romping through the woods. He came back an hour later, wet and panting, with a dead brown squirrel in his mouth. 'You don't want that,' I told him. 'Release.' On the way back toward town, we stopped at a pet store. There was nothing on the shelves that didn't look small and pathetic. Finally I chose a thick rawhide bone. In the car, I gave it to him. 'I'm sorry,' I said.

I drove to the animal shelter. The girl at the desk asked me to fill out a card with my name and Uno's. My hand trembled like a nervous kid, like when I was ten years old at the free throw line and my father would scream 'No pressure! No pressure!' from the sideline. Uno prowled around the room, sniffing. Then he heard the distant barking of other dogs, and he yelped questioningly.

'Will he get gassed?' I asked.

'A dog this pretty? No problem. Some family will come pick him up tomorrow morning.' She leaned down to stroke Uno's fur. 'You're a pretty boy, aren't you? You sure are.' Uno leaned hard against her scratching, then leapt up and began licking the girl's chin.

'Hey,' she said, laughing. 'Hey, sweet boy. Settle down.'

'Fine,' I said. 'Do I need to sign anything?'

The girl looked up at me and shook her head. 'Do you want to say goodbye?' she asked. 'I mean, alone?' Uno looked at me, grinning.

'I've done that already,' I said. I put my hand on Uno's soft yellow forehead, and I left.

When I came home it was late, and Christina was asleep, her hair a dark cloud on the pillow. I undressed silently and climbed in next to her, rolled onto my side and closed my eyes.

After a few moments she put her hand on my shoulder. 'Honey?' she asked. I didn't move.

'Oh, baby,' she said. 'Oh, baby.'

In the days after I dropped Uno off I received sympathy. Grown men shook their heads and muttered. *Damn shame.* I shuffled slowly from the bedroom to the kitchen, to the bathroom, to the family room. 'Thank you,' Christina said, 'what else can I say? When are you going to cut it out?'

I cracked open cold cans of Busch and sat in a lawn chair, alone.

'Go ahead, be angry at me for being pregnant,' she called, from the family room. 'There's a part of me that feels sorry for you, Cooper, but not much. Can you understand that?'

I didn't answer.

'You exaggerate, is what you do. You talk through your ass

half the time, honey. But there's no one here to listen to you: it's just you and me.'

'I can't hear you,' I shouted. 'I can't hear a word you're saying.'

Christina's water broke two weeks before Doctor Fang said it would. Our neighbour, Loretta, called me at the plant and told me Christina was on the way to Crittenton, and that I should get my ass over there, pronto.

I took the call in Jerry's office. 'Go,' he told me. 'Go. Go.'

I nearly flooded my Mustang, but then I was on Walton, trying to drive. The world seemed incredibly quiet, and I felt the need to talk to everything - my car, the stoplights, other drivers - urging them on. The hospital is a fourteen minute drive from the plant, and as I moved with the afternoon traffic I remembered that Christina had known immediately that it would be a boy.

'How do you know?' I'd scoffed. 'How can you possibly know something like that?'

She'd said, 'Because I'm a woman, Cooper. You forget that sometimes.'

At the entrance to the hospital I nearly T-boned a brown Oldsmobile, I stood on the brakes while an older man gave me the finger, but then I was jogging across the vast parking lot toward the front doors. My chest felt light and huge, but achy, like it was a big balloon that someone was sticking their finger into. I tried to steady myself. The speed was inside me, wild and uncontrolled, as if there was no driver. It lifted me up and carried me through the front doors, past the reception desk, and up three floors to my wife, who was already puffing rhythmically, in and out, the way Sandy had taught us.

In one month, Michael will be two. At night, in our bedroom, Christina and I bicker in hushed tones. We argue about what's best for him. *Him.* He sits on my knee and looks at me, wanting to know things, and I tell him. I teach him everything I know.

16

Martin Malone

Runner-up in the 1996/97 Fish Short Story Prize

I live on the edge of the Curragh Plains with Bernadette, Colin (14)
and Barry (4). I took up writing for something to do. When I was
thirteen, I wrote some stories called *Rob Royton*. I keep the last surviving
one as a memento of a character I really liked, but killed off for some
reason I forget.

Most hurtful thing about writing: people laughing at stories you penned
to be serious stuff, and sitting grim faced at would-be comedy stories.

Best thing: When it all comes together.

Black George

Martin Malone

He came from the hills of Antrim and spoke in a thick Northern Ireland accent from the corner of his mouth, as if everything he said was confidential, a secret he was parting with for your ears alone.

He wore suits, always dark like spoiled clouds, and they were never without creases. He was taller than Dad; then, as Black George said, everyone with legs under his behind stood taller than Dad.

We'd wake on Friday mornings, and Black George would be sitting at our table chasing a rasher around the plate. His apple cheeks freshly washed and shaved, his teeth in, his dark eyes like washed lumps of coal, he'd say 'Morning men.'

He'd lick his fingers after eating and Mum would be standing over the frying pan, her lips tight, refusing to reprimand Dad's friend, but reprimanding him through us for a habit not ours.

Dad brought home lots of friends during the racing season. He'd meet them under the stand at the racecourse or in the pub. Mum said every hungry stray in the place followed him home.

Once he brought home a German doctor and his wife who smoked rolled up cigarettes that left a heavy smell in the air. They sang *Silent Night* in German a couple of times. Mum didn't like the

19

woman, the way her short skirt gave little peeps of her pink underwear. Dad never complained, nor did Black George who kept nudging Mum every time the skirt gave a little rise, as if Mum was interested. Dad also brought home a jockey called Hagan. He'd red hair and a sad face primed to cry. His lips were almost absent from his face, turned inwards, as if kissing the hurting that was going on inside. Black George loved the Curragh. He said the scent of the furze was like an air freshener in his lungs. Dad'd nod when he'd say things like that. They never spoke about politics. Not even when things got rough in the North, and Black George drew strange looks in the *Railway Arms*. On Sundays a man with a kind face but hard eyes would drop a banned pamphlet at the tables, and wait for a small donation to land on his palm. Most fed him something no matter how small. But Black George grew quiet and stared at his drink, as if a dozen snakes were standing beside him. Dad's smile, his ready quips diffused the situation, but he never brought Black George back.

That's the story he spun Mum when Black George missed a couple of race meetings. He'd ring to say something had come up, and Dad would nod, give an understanding sigh, because he liked the big man, and say okay.

Meanwhile Dad continued to attend the meetings. He did well from gambling; it was as if his happy-go-lucky disposition was adored by the Gods. But he'd never admit to being lucky. How could it be luck, he'd say, after hours spent studying the horses' track records, and weeding sense from the horse whispers that flooded the town. People in town were always giving tips; 'this is a certainty... or this is a sure thing... it's flying I tell you.' Dad had an uncanny knack of knowing what a horse was capable of. But a run of bad luck, while not diminishing his smile, forced him into accepting the post of foreman at a stable. Looking on the bright side, he told Black George over the phone, that he needed a source of inside information.

Black George owned a factory somewhere up North, outside

his beloved Antrim. He'd arrive in with trays of unwrapped chocolate bars, and tell us to get stuck in. Mum'd smile, and ask how he was, and did he marry yet, and Black George's beetle black eyebrows would give a small lift, and his mouth a jaded sigh.

Black George said she couldn't hack the weather, and the tension up North she found unsettling, which he thought was rich coming from a Lebanese. Granted, he said, an American Lebanese. We only saw her once, and she looked nothing like Dad had described. A woman as tall as Black George she was leaning towards heaviness. She didn't appear to be interested in meeting people; the sort no sooner sitting down than they want to be on the move again.

While Black George was absent from the racing circuit, Dad brought home another friend. A vet. This man wore thick glasses. He was short and chubby faced, and like George he wore suits, except his were lighter in colour. He'd a deep voice, and the sort of eyes you see every now and then in a clear summer sky.

He liked to sing after a few drinks. *Michael Row The Boat Ashore*, and another about a train always being late. He sang other songs, too. Rebel ballads about Pearse and Connolly. Songs Dad knew, but sang half-heartedly, because he said he didn't like guns and bullets, and that killing or dying by them was nothing to sing about. He told Liam that, and the vet rubbed his balding head, and nodded. Black George arrived down after a few weeks. He said he wanted to buy a racehorse. Dad asked was he interested in buying into a partnership with a friend of his who'd just bought a grey colt. Black George hesitated. He'd lost a little weight, which Mum said proved how lost he was without his love. Dad said he'd given up eating his own chocolate bars. Black George smiled. A worried little smile that painted a picture for Dad he didn't like. That his friend's mind ached.

Black George liked the horse if not Liam. Dad said the partnership was a bad idea from the start. Liam was a true green

Republican and Black George a true Orange Loyalist. When Dad was merry he berated the two of them; saying the horse wouldn't be called *Rebel Pride*, or *Orange Parade*, but *All Friends*.

The horse won three races, but neither Black George nor Liam - Mum called him Green Liam - ever stood in the parade ring together. And the partnership was broken up after a row at home when Liam said something in Irish, and got a shock when Black George understood, and told him quietly but fiercely that there was a million guns in a million homes up North... all saying NO.

Dad got vexed then, with the two of them, and put Liam out, telling him to cool down and get sense.

Then he rounded on Black George, not for what he'd said, but for rising to the bait, and losing his cool. Black George, standing head and shoulders above Dad, shrugged, and spread his hands in embarrassment.

Liam phoned afterwards and said he was sorry, that it had been drink talk, and how was he to know that Black George understood Irish.

The winter set in, and we didn't see much of Black George. He sent a card for Christmas and a box of chocolates. He'd ring Dad now and then, and Dad would return the calls.

Black George said he'd be at Leopardstown on Boxing Day. Dad said he'd go if he could bring Liam. Black George went silent and then said the 'yes', that probably saved his life.

It was in a pub after the races that it happened. A man followed Black George and Dad into the toilets. A pistol was produced against Black George's neck. Dad went outside and got Liam who accompanied him to the toilets. Liam rapped the door, spoke harshly about Black George being a friend. Afterwards, with Black George trembling like a leaf about to be wind blown, Liam apologised, 'the reg. number of your car made them suspicious. I'm sorry.' Dad told Mum all this with disgust etched on his face. But that episode was lost amongst the other things that happened.

Mum and Dad weren't getting along. Arguments broke out over ridiculous things. They no longer shared the same bedroom, and when I walked into the kitchen one day, ready with the news that I was taking Dad's advice and heading to New York, the atmosphere was charged.

It took a short while to find out why. Mum suspected Dad of having an affair with a younger, much younger woman. I don't know the truth of it. But a couple of months after I'd left for America Dad rang to say he'd moved down country. And Mum called the same evening. She put a brave voice on things, and said he'd be back when he thought things over.

Mum liked to write, but Dad preferred to phone. He kept me informed about Black George. Told me that Black George's teenage daughter was killed by a hit-and-run driver. Black George had never married, he said, without going into the depths of the matter.

Dad attended the funeral. He said it was such a waste of young life. Black George kept away from the people who'd been prominent in rearing his daughter. He didn't reveal much outward emotion; eyes squinted, and lips caught in a grimace. No tears. Not one, Dad said.

Green Liam had cancer, and was given six months to live. He doesn't see anyone, not even Dad. He has it in the face, Dad said. I suspect Dad met Phil in Antrim. He was travelling up and down in an effort to help Black George. Seems the only time the big man opened up was when the two of them nursed a whiskey bottle during the night. He'd cry sometimes then and talk about his daughter. The Lebanese American came back into his life but Black George wasn't interested. Dad didn't tell me about Black George's whiskey tears or the Lebanese American, but Black George himself when he visited me in Woodside on a freezing Christmas Eve. The two of us welcomed Christmas Dawn with a bottle of Chivas Regal and twin puffs of cigar smoke.

He admired the photographs of Dad I had on the wall. Dad and his chestnut Dream Horse, and the pair snapped mid-air over a Punchestown fence. Black George had lost more weight, and the red flush was now a dangerous purple on his cheeks.

Black George spoke in the low tones of a depressed man. The twinkle of humour was clouded over in his eyes. He managed a smile when I reminded him of the time he pencilled over the Pope's eye in a newspaper photograph, and of Green Liam singing *Amhran Na Bhlian*, and he *God save the Queen*, simultaneously, and the two of them twisted and holding each other up, desecrating the words of both songs with slurred and giggling voices.

Black George nodded, and stared into his drink while telling me Green Liam had died the night before last. Black George had business in town, dismantling a business partnership or something with his ex-Lebanese American intended. The night before he left he treated me to a Chinese meal, and mentioned Phil to me, about how much happier Dad was since meeting her. Black George pressed a few notes into my palm, and wouldn't hear tell of my refusing his money, 'you're only getting on your feet, lad... maybe you'll want to come home in the summer.'

I watched him leaving in the yellow cab. The money he'd given me was a decent sum, and I remembered that Black George always had a generous streak in his bones; was always giving me and my brothers pocket money, and chocolate bars from his factory. He bailed Green Liam out of trouble, too. But he'd never admit to that, had told Dad that it was a debt repaid.

Mum called shortly afterwards in near hysteria. Dad was living with someone down south. The shame of it, she said. I asked her was it not the loss of him. And she said quietly, 'that too.'

I met Dad and Black George in the summer at a Curragh race meeting as planned. The sky was blue and the gambled-on horse didn't mar the good day. Black George was, if not back to himself, then as close to it as he had been for a long time. Dad was relaxed, and in good humour. He asked me to go see him riding in

24

a vet's race in Tipperary, and I did.

Black George drove. It was his horse Dad was riding. Oh, it hadn't a hope in hell, he said, but he'd stick a few quid on it each way. The horse finished third, and between Dad's youthful glow and Black George's burst of smiling, you'd think the pair of them had just performed a miracle or something. Dad said they were just sharing the magic of a sport they loved.

Black George gave me a loan of his car to drop Dad down the country. He was heading back north on the train after staying overnight in bed and breakfast. He'd company, that's why he didn't want to come with us. A blonde woman with freckles. Black George said he liked her because she reminded him of the German doctor's wife.

I met Phil in Dad's house, and got along with her after a somewhat nervous accidental introduction on Dad's behalf. Later that night I'd to tell Mum that Dad wouldn't be coming home. Not ever.

Black George said the blonde girl was a disappointment. If she'd underwear like the German doctor's wife he never found out. Shortly afterwards Black George sold his business. He was on about moving to Scotland and marrying a widow he'd met through a dating agency. She was an artist, he said, and a good one, too. Dad thought he was joking again, and didn't think anymore of it until a gilt-edged wedding invitation dropped in his letterbox.

Dad rang me to let me know how the occasion had gone. Rained all day, he said, and a bitter bone scraping wind blew. But the weather didn't blunt the smiles on the faces of Black George and his new wife, who Dad said bore an uncanny resemblance to the Lebanese American.

Gloria. Black Gloria, Dad called her, was just what his friend needed in his life. She'd a veneer of toughness covering a kind heart. He was saddened a little that Black George was finished with Curragh race days, and when the two of them sang For The

Good Times at the wedding reception, Gloria said that perhaps they should have married each other.

I didn't see Black George for a long time afterwards. Not until Phil rang and broke the news to me about Dad. And then we met at the funeral.

Hagan was there, his lips no longer kissing his hurt. Red hair slicked and polished. He'd a new woman on his arm. He said Dad was there for him when his saddle was soapy.

Black George, wrinkled up clothes matching his wrinkled-up eyes, grimaced. He was heavier than I remembered. Gloria was taking good care of him. You could see that, the way she stood beside him, squeezing his hand.

Afterwards in a bar where I'd arranged refreshments Black George nursed a large brandy. Gloria and Phil were having a chat; Phil semi-listening and semi-taking in Gloria's soft touches.

Black George had tears in his eyes, but they were gone in a couple of snuffles and a bite on his lower lip. He said if I needed anything to let him know. Said that my father was a sound man, a real friend. One who didn't mind getting his shoes wet for you. He put his hand on my shoulder, and then walked away. I never saw him again.

About five years later Gloria wrote. Her name took a moment to register. Her letter was short and to the point. Black George, she wrote, died on February 4th at home in Edinburgh after a brief illness. He'd wanted me to have something - a picture to hang on my wall with the others he'd seen. A painting of three men. Recognisable to me. They're in a parade ring, all smiles, all with cigars. And the caption underneath in dark bold reads 'All Friends'.

Alex Keegan

Runner-up in the 1996/97 Fish Short Story Prize

Born 1947. Mother Irish, father Welsh - inherited the bad halves.
Parents split when he was eight - children's homes, fostered, all
unhappily. Left school unqualified, RAF, court marshalled 1969 for
refusing punishment. Read Evan Hunter's *Mothers and Daughters* while
'inside', which rekindled desire for reading / writing. Many jobs, garage
hand, clerk, sold sports gear, drove taxis, TV engineer, double-glazing
salesman, sales manager.
Studied psychology, Liverpool. Drifted into computers. Injured Clapham
Rail Crash 1988. *Alleged* hero. Suffered Post Traumatic Stress. Became
house-husband.
Winner Raconteur. Bridport Prize supplementary winner 1996. Author
of Caz Flood Mysteries - *Cuckoo* 1994, *Vulture* 1995, *Kingfisher*
1995, *Razorbill* 1996. Fifth novel, *A Wild Justice* to be published
by Piatkus, July 1997.

Tomatoes, Flamingos, Lemmings, and Other Interesting Facts

Alex Keegan

I always think, you know, it's like being on stage. You have to look your best. You come in from the wings and there's your audience and straight away you're in the spotlight, you can't hide, and every night you have to perform, no matter what. You've been short-changed on the maintenance again and the kids need new shoes, maybe it's that time of the month and you're feeling shit, but you have to do it, you do, look good for the punters. It's yer job.

I nearly went stripping once, but at the last minute, I bottled out. I thought that being behind a bar would be easier. I've been here for two years, one month, a week and a half; five quid an hour, tips and a conveyor belt of blokes. I think I should've gone stripping.

The lights, you know, it's one kind of glamorous, especially early on in the evening, when the smoke's not too bad and the blokes are still close to being reasonable. When you first come in, you can't smell the beer or the fag-ash. They clean the place with some special stuff that's got a really strong perfume and they've brassed up the taps. For a while, you feel really great.

The blokes that come in early, they're either the old fellahs, or guys on their way home from work. The old fellahs, they'll use my name and smile. Sometimes they'll call me luv but in a nice sort of way.

'My usual, Amy.'

'Half a Mack's luv.'

'Hello, Amy, how's the best-looking girl in Brighton?'

Later on, you get the serious drinkers, the leches an' the young lads who drink too fast like they want to hurt themselves. They're the worst, the lads, they talk like rapists. There's something cold and nasty in their eyes even if it is only the drink. They say the most horrible, the dirtiest things sometimes. Sometimes, if it gets really out of hand, the landlord'll say something but most of the time we're expected to cope. 'Call it water offa duck's back and just keep serving,' Bill says. So that's what we do.

Sometimes you get a chance to say something funny, but you have to be so careful nowadays. Young blokes, they've got no honour. They'd hit an old man, two or three on one, so what's a barwoman to them? As far as they're concerned, we're all slags. They haven't got a clue. I know it's the drink talking but they still haven't got a clue. I wonder sometimes if they've got mothers. I just don't know...

You get chatted up all the time. A nice bloke does it, maybe I'll go out with him but only if I've laid down the law first. I've had marriage - and sex, well I can take it or leave it. I tell 'em before we go out, but they never believe me. They believe me when I do say goodnight on the door though, just like I said I would. Girls should have the choice, right?

So when this bloke came in one night, not a regular, asked for a 6X and then said there was magic in my face, light in my eyes, I was a bit taken back, you know, like you would be.

'You what?' I said. He smiled at me. 'I said you've got a nice face.'

'Tell me something I don't know,' I said.

'Tomatoes,' he said, 'people used to think they were poisonous.'

'What?' I said.

'People thought you couldn't eat tomatoes. They thought they were poisonous.'

It was fairly quiet so I said, 'I knew that.'

'Knew what?'

'Tomatoes. Poisonous.'

'But they're not,' he said.

'Some of 'em might be.'

'My name's Frank,' he said.

He went then and I didn't see him for days. That night, after tilling up and wiping down, I had a brandy with Bill. I wanted to ask him if he knew this Frank, but I didn't. I kept thinking about him but I couldn't picture his face, except that it was pale. I didn't sleep all that well. In the morning, my flatmate Mary did us both a fry-up. She asked me if I wanted tomatoes.

'No thanks,' I said. 'Did you know they used to think they were poisonous?'

'Who did?' Mary said.

'Did what?'

'Thought tomatoes?'

I should have asked Frank that but I never thought.

'Everyone,' I said.

'Bollocks,' she said.

Frank came in again about two weeks later. He was wearing jeans, a donkey jacket and that slightly off-centred smile.

I said, 'Pint?'

He said, 'There are more plastic flamingos in the world than real ones.'

'Fascinating,' I said.

'Fancy trying the other side of the bar some time?' he said.

'No,' I said.

When I told Mary, (about the flamingos), she said, 'Who says?'

31

I told her, 'Me. I counted them.'

A week before my thirty-seventh birthday he came in again, a white-haired bim on his arm with licensed tits.

'Pint?' I said.

'Please,' he said.

'And what about your mother?' I said.

I served 'em. They went away. I couldn't quite see them but I heard him once, laughing at something dirty, then her, hee-hawing like a ship's boiler.

When he came back to the bar, I asked, 'Is your mother not well?'

'Did you know,' he said, 'that lemmings are afraid of heights?'

'Yes,' I said, 'and did *you* know that in this country *alone,* an average of seventy-two people every day die while they're taking a crap?'

'How many is that world-wide?' he said.

I was best part of thirty-eight next time I saw him. He came in with a thing about fifteen, plain brown hair but the spit of her mother.

'Got time to talk?' he said.

'No,' I said, 'too much to do.'

'Shame,' he said. 'I was rather hoping you were ready to hop the bar.'

'Busy!' I said. 'Pint?'

'Please,' he said, 'and a coke for my niece.'

'Oh, p-ll-eease...' I said. His *niece?* I couldn't help myself.

'What d'you mean?' the little bim said to me. 'This is my Uncle Frank. You've met my Mum already.'

Frank grinned. 'Did you know,' he said, 'that Oscar Wilde wanted to be a professional footballer?'

'What club?' I said.

Then he asked me, he said, 'Can you fall in love in

instalments?' I gave him a pint, a coke and best part of a smile.

'Well?' he said.

I leaned forward. His eyes were blue. He pursed his lips.

'Ask me next time you're in,' I said.

I'm thirty-nine tomorrow. Frank's promised to come in. He's going to get me pregnant tonight. His niece is baby-sitting my Davey and we're going over to Worthing for a night at the dogs. I fancy a curry after and then a drive up the Downs. Did you know there's enough chalk under the Downs to supply every teacher for the next billion years? That's not just the UK, that's every teacher, every teacher in the whole world.

The universe probably.

Tim Booth

Runner-up in the 1996/97 Fish Short Story Prize

Born in Kill, 1943, educated all over, graduated TCD. A subsequent meaningful life-enhancing year as an advertising spook felt like it might force a mature career decision, so left to play music with Dr. Strangely Strange. The three chord trick. Two albums recorded - *Kip of the Serenes* 1968, and *Heavy Petting* 1970. Nobody - apart from a dangerous band of Neo Post Modernists on the north side of Reykjavik - was taken in, so the band split up - *do-wah* - but still occasionally get together. Third album recently recorded, twenty-five years in gestation - *The Difficult Third Album*. These days - what remains of them - a film maker, artist and designer, lurking on the edge of the Wicklow hills, or some place like Clonakilty. Dangerous when roused.

Compound Interest written for my children, Jesse and Rayne, and as a prologue to a novel entitled *Altergeist*.

There's no fool like an old fool.

Compound Interest

Tim Booth

Here's me - on a wall over near Cookstown - sitting and waiting. Some pony. I hated being out in the open like that, in full view. I couldn't hunch down any lower, because, even then, I was seriously big, but I had to act casual, like I had a natural right to be there. I'd heard the stories. You could be mugged - killed for a laugh - out in those badlands, because there were no rules outside the Compounds, and God knows what style of gouger might have been on the prowl that evening. But I had to do it. I had to. I chanced a look around.

Behind me, the burnt-out garda station was a web of wreckage against the evening sun. That had gone up in the first weeks of fighting - brewed up - the old law and order smashed down by newfangled RPGs. Now all seemed quiet. Nothing moving, no chance random factors. I'd be safe enough, it was too early for the gangs to be out yet.

I'd chosen my position carefully, hidden in behind the husk of a rusting double-decker, but with a clear view of the deserted by-pass. It looked great - all shimmery in the evening light - two long ribbons of tarmac, laid out like they'd been dropped across the curve of the world by a careless giant. I just had to wait - like the boys waiting for Godot - staring down the road, passing the time

35

by picking white flakes of old paint from the brickwork. Flakes like petals of dry skin. There were a lot of bad diseases going round those days. Still are, for that matter.

A half-track full of AMCO soldiers came hammering down the road, bucked across the central divide and roared away towards Jobstown, aerials whipping, sniffing the air like cockroach feelers, looking for a taste of something rotten. I watched it swing around the wreckage of the footbridge, a mess of twisted metal jutting into the road. Good riddance. AMCO squaddies, spam-fed Yankee doodlers out on patrol, little black eyes under the big helmets, whacked up on wiz, shoot you soon as look at you. But they weren't looking for me that time.

The machine scuttled in behind a row of collapsed houses and disappeared behind the ruined mall. That place must have been mega before the war. Nana said it was the biggest shopping centre on the south side, but poor old Nana said lots of stupid things - when she could remember them.

I pulled the army greatcoat in against the wind. The CD Roms clicked together in the inside pocket. That's why I was out there. I'd be able to trade them. Big Ted was crazy for Nineties art softs, and I'd barter them for that box of watercolours Ripper had told me about. Maybe get some good paper as well. Hard to find, but Ted's your man for that type of thing, so Ripper said. Where was he, anyway? He was supposed to be over by four, and it was gone half past.

The sun had got low, long shadows out across the road. There were clouds up on the hills like pink cotton wool, almost hiding the burnt patches. Blackened scrub, wounds from the war. Russian guns positioned up there during the siege, lobbing shells into the heart of the city - you could still see the napalm scars left over from the AMCO air strikes, I'd gone up once, years ago, and the smell would turn your stomach. Nana almost ate me alive when I got back, said the whole place was full of mines. Half the kids on my street had only one foot.

A big car lashed past on the road. I watched it go - a Zim stretch full of Russian sky pilots - stopping for nothing. Windows blacked out so you couldn't look in. Or out. Who'd want to? All they'd have seen would be ruins, miles of them, twisted scrap, plastic bags blown by the wind like mute tumbleweed, gangs of scrawny dogs poking in the rubbish, and over beyond the old concrete plant, the rusting steel wall guarding Firhouse Compound, watchtowers and searchlights stuck up in the setting sun. I lived in there. Me and Nana - when she could remember to come home - in two rooms of a damp corpo house, windows boarded over, but by then, I was used to working by artificial light. God be with the Compound generator, and the divine light of Diesel. Jesus, where had Ripper got to? It'd be curfew at half seven, and that wouldn't leave much time.

That could be him now. Two huge eighteen wheelers were coming up the hill under a cloud of black smoke, big high sided containers lashed to the flatbeds. They'd be full of Japanese goodies on their way to the neo-yuppie wet dream that was Bless'ton Compound: food processors, computers, Taiwan whiskey, hair dryers, Parker Knoll recliners; fancy crap for the Compound dwellers, too rich and too afraid to come into the city any more. Afraid of what they might find. Or who might just find them. Bit like myself really, scared of the big wide world, that blind wilderness of ruins between the safe havens of the Compounds. It shouldn't have been like that. Fuck the war.

A low Hummer jeep swung out from behind the first truck, missile pods sticking up like mickies. Guarding the lorries from the Jackers up above in Jobstown, protecting their valuable cargoes. The jeep bounced past, Spacehopper tyres scrunching grit, V8 howling - I loved that - like an image from a book. The first truck lumbered away as the second changed down with a scrunch of cogs. Driver missed his gears - wanker - the truck slowing up as if something had distracted it. A dark shape came off the lorry's arse end, and swung across the roadway in a blur of arms and legs, rollerblades slicing the tarmac. That was him - the skate boy.

'Over here, Ripper.'

I was on my feet, yelling into the noise. He moved away from the convoy, sprinted across the carriage way, and up the slip road that used lead to the station. He braked to a stop in a clatter of small stones, panting, grinning at me, eyes deep in the sockets of his skull. Wasted.

'Did you see that? Only way to travel, Robbo my man.'

Nana would have cut my balls off if I'd done that. Hanging out the back of the big supply truck like a demented bat, rollerblades smoking from the speed, hitching a ride.

'You're some pony, Ripper, you know that? Come on the fuck, it's late, and Big Ted will close up if we don't move.' I used my grown-up voice, but he wasn't impressed.

'Don't sweat it - I called him earlier. He'll stay open - Ivan Bollix - he knows we're the business.' He pulled at the rucksack slung across his back. 'Not late, am I? Bit of aggro over in 'Laoghaire Mart. That fucker Eamon - never knows which side of his bread is greased.' Rubbing a hand through his shorn hair. I'd have loved to get mine cut like that. A bit of style.

'You got what you wanted?' I asked.

'I got what I *needed* all right, but it wasn't what Eamo wanted - know what I mean?' A bleak smile, like a fridge door opening. I wasn't going to ask. Ripper'd been on the streets a long time and you don't survive if you're stupid. I just nodded. I knew well what he meant. Nana said Ripper got that name during the fighting, surviving on his wits when everyone else was starving. He'd used a little red Swiss army knife to skin rats: traded their pelts and flesh in the long winter siege, and God knows what else he'd done. These days he lived to trade - and to skate. Always had the best gear.

He pulled up the zip on his leather jacket, and bent to adjust the strapping of his blades. Not new, but much better than most - Nike's - must have cost a fortune. He straightened, all skinny and black against the light.

'Come on,' he said, 'Warp factor nine. Engage.' Moving out from the wall, kicking his long legs, blades grinding in the dirt, arms swinging, he skated away from me, and I had to run after him, my coat flapping in the wind, slowing me up. I hated that.

He was moving easily through the ruins, and I felt real stupid, lumbering behind him like one of those mutie fuckers they said lived in near the city centre. A centre that was now a huge flooded crater known as The Burn - the whole area along the Liffey a fused wasteland, taken out years ago by a so-called clean tac-nuke - rad sickness spreading out through the flattened suburbs like an invisible smell. What did they call it? A half life. Radiation with a half life of a hundred zillion years - lasts forever - seeping under your door like a hungry ghost. Maybe that's what was affecting me. Fucking half life, when all I wanted was a whole one. When would I ever stop growing? I was six foot eleven then, and it was getting real hard finding clothes to fit. Maybe Big Ted could help. Maybe he'd have something for a sixteen year old giant who wanted to be the next Robert Ballagh. That's if we ever got to Ted's in the first place. Jesus Ripper, slow down. He'd stopped at a junction of two roads, waving back at me. I was running, doing my best, but I was near knackered. Only one lung.

There were ruined factories all around. Old shops, showroom windows lying in pools of plastic that had run hot across the rubble, then cooled into weird shapes, like some sort of poisonous ice. Before the war this used be the Cookstown trading estate.

We moved past the twisted buildings, some blown apart at the seams - corrugated metal sheets flung like rusty playing cards across the road - others blackened by fire, their walls sagging, melted from the inside. I'd have loved to draw them - make a great background for one of those *beat 'em up* games - the whole place felt like it had been hit by an earthquake, concrete paths cracked and blistered, clumps of nettles and strange magenta flowers sprouting everywhere. Graffiti on the walls, spray canned messages that claimed the territory for one or other of the night gangs. *Casanova Okay, Kip of the Serenes, Mary Malones of Moscow.* I'd never be able to find my way in there again, and if Nana'd known where I was, she'd have thrown a fit. She often had fits - said it was to do with the stuff the Russians used during the war. Poly somethings. Eyes rolled up into her wrinkled old head, and a terrible green dribble out of her nose, like a child with a snotty cold, only it's not a cold, some sort of a fever. Nana said it was a sin-drome, whatever that was. Gulf War sin-drome. You got it from breathing the air.

The air where we were was better though. We moved along the edge of an overgrown park, all wild yellow grasses, and mutie blackberry clumps, trees hacked down to stumps for firewood. Somebody had tied a billy goat to a breeze block, and the animal stared at me like it couldn't believe its eyes. Ahead there was another factory, only this one had most of its roof. An old Skoda was parked outside, its body rotten with rust. The factory door was rusty as well, a big slab of orange steel welded onto girders set into the concrete. Looked strong enough to stop an anti-tank. Up above it, a little camera - the size of your willy - swivelled to follow our movement. Ripper braked to a halt in the big empty space in front of the building. It had been cleared of rubble to give an uninterrupted field of fire. No place to hide there. I didn't like the feel of it, never liked being exposed.

'Jesus, Ripper, we're too late - the gaff's closed.'

'Not at all, Robbo, relax. That's just what Big Ted wants you to think. Don't worry, he's in there all right.' He was kneeling, taking off his blades. He got a worn pair of runners from his knapsack and slipped them on, then stood again, the rollerblades dangling from each hand. He held them up to the little camera.

'Ted. You Russian Bollix. Open up. It's me, Ripper, and I've brought a friend. We've come to trade.'

'I can see that. Are you sure you weren't followed?' A voice crackled from a speaker set into the door behind an armoured grill.

'Of course I'm sure - think I'm stupid? Let's in. It's cold out here.'

The door opened. Behind it, a dark corridor. Abandon hope.

'Come on Robbo,' Ripper grinned, 'we're in.'

The corridor was maybe thirty feet long. I ducked my head in under the door. It sealed behind me with a thud and lights came on. I felt like a rat in a trap, but Ripper moved confidently down the passage to a hanging flap of dirty plastic covering the far exit. He pushed through and I followed him in.

I couldn't hardly believe my eyes.

It was huge. A dimly lit warehouse, the whole place stacked floor to ceiling with incredible piles of strange things - spilling everywhere - like some kind of mute Aladdin's cave. I tried to take it in, but it was too much. Sensory overload. Where would I start? Rolls of carpet, pieces of cars, half a helicopter, doors, radiator grills, a gilded antique mirror, old paintings, stacks of rusting washing machines - their insides spilled out like elephant guts - rows of dusty televisions, bicycles hung up by their front wheels from the ceiling. Dust sheets thrown over strangely angled machinery, stacks of ammunition crates, racks and racks of oily spare parts, piles of crockery, pine tables and dressers sagging under the weight of large cardboard boxes, Japanese symbols stencilled onto their sides. Brand names: Panasonic, Sony, Smith and Wesson, Oil of Ulay, Rolyflex, Calvin Klein, Mitsubishi. Everything covered with a thick layer of dirt, cobwebs like tattered lace swinging from the roof beams, greasy strip lighting on dirty chains, oil and water puddling the concrete floor.

'Welcome to Big Ted's,' Ripper said, hands on his skinny hips, gazing about in admiration. 'Ted! I see you've been spring cleaning. The place looks great!'

'Very funny, Skater. You'll need to take a more humble approach if you wish to haggle with me today.'

I looked around, but I couldn't see anybody. The voice came

41

from the middle of the biggest stack of junk. Ripper moved over to it, and peered past a heap of used tyres into a small wooden cubicle - an old garden shed - that had been almost totally covered by the piles of trade goods. Above the door in a gold frame was a picture I thought I recognised - all big brush strokes - a lad with his hands over his ears and his mouth wide open like he was howling at the moon. Had to be a repro. A counter was laid across the open door, and behind it on a plush office chair, sat the strangest little man.

'Robbo. May I present Big Ted. The magpie man. Collector of art and purveyor of goods to the needy.' Ripper laughed. His teeth were very white, but Nana said they were his own. Another of her stories.

'Big Ted?' I was confused. I had imagined him to be bigger, huge, what with a name like that. He was tiny, like an elf, his face all one toothless grin - a smiling walnut.

'Good evening Robbo.' Big Ted eyed me up in a glittery sort of way. 'Pay no attention to your friend. I may be small in stature, but fortunately, there is a part of me - a most agreeable commodity - that is unnaturally large, and that was how I obtained my name.'

'Star of stage and screen - vid porn out of Riga before the war, wasn't it Ted?' Ripper was pushing his luck. The man seemed to change colour, blushing as if somebody had shone a red light on his bald head.

'That's as maybe. Now. What can I do you for lads?'

'You still got that old box of paints?' Ripper's voice like silk. I pulled out the CD Roms. 'Robbo here would like to trade you for it - fancies himself as a bit of a Jackson, know what I mean?'

The little man's eyes were like staples into my soul.

'So, you think you're an artist, do you? That's an interesting conceit, these times, in one so young, and... so very big. Are you any good?'

'He's the best,' Ripper said. I didn't know how to deal with that.

'That so?' Big Ted's smile was all gums. 'Perhaps you'd like to prove your friend's belief in you.' He climbed down from his chair and went into the hut. I could see pictures on the walls in there. A big canvas of a little old fashioned girl with a sort of hula hoop, surrounded by loads of dressed up people in a park, and one of those Russian jobs, all gold leaf and a woman praying, her head on one side and her eyes rolled up in her face as if she was on E.

He came back out with a pad of beautiful grainy paper, and a chipped black box, all sort of flat. He put it up on the counter, opened it, and there they were. A full set of Winsor and Newton watercolours from before the war - like I had only dreamed about - each colour fixed like a gum drop in its little white container. He poured half a bottle of designer water into a greasy beaker, and held out a fistful of brushes. 'If you think you're so good, fellow-me-lad, I'll set you a task while your friend and I have a little commercial discussion.'

'What?' I said. Ripper was nodding and smiling, like he knew something I didn't.

'It's simple.' The Russian explained, 'Draw me. That's all you have to do. If you show any talent - which I seriously doubt - the paints are yours. If not...' His eyes took on a nightmare look. '. . . then you will owe me a very special favour.' He clenched his fist on the little snub of his arm, and I had a bad, bad feeling, but I took the box of colours all the same. I'd show them.

The rest of the evening sort of passed me by. I'm like that when I work. The paints were fantastic. They fell off the brush like quicksilver, and I could control the washes in a way that I had never even imagined. Compared with the crude colours I made for myself at Nana's, these were like the ultimate painting machines. Far better than the best software programmes, these paints actually liked water, and loved the paper. And God knows where Ted had come by the brushes. I know now that they were sable, the very best.

I drew Ted, with pale sepia using a fine brush, filled in the highlights with a gentle wash of yellow, leaving the paper come through like I always knew it would. Then laid in his skin tone, building up the shadow areas with darker washes. Every time I needed something - fresh water, a pencil, a razor blade to scrape back another highlight - Ted just put it on the counter in front of me. I don't know how long it took, but I used all the paper, cutting each sheet from the block, to find another one beneath, pre-stretched and ready for me. Each sketch got better and better. When Ted and Ripper moved away to do some kind of a barter, I drew the place itself, adding in everything I knew from my limited skills. Hours must have passed, but I was on another planet.

At last, a hand fell across my shoulders. I looked up. I hadn't realised it, but I was down on my knees in the middle of the warehouse, the pad before me on the dusty floor, drawings spilling out around me like fallen leaves.

'You can stop now, lad.' The Russian was gazing down at me, and I swear his little eyes were all wet. 'You've made your point.'

Ripper was leaning against a stack of old bed frames beside Ted's office, calm and relaxed, pleased with himself. I was coming back into the real world slowly, trying to get a grip. The little Russian gathered up the drawings, and leafed through them, nodding to himself.

'Good,' he said, 'very good. You can keep the paints and brushes.' I couldn't believe him.

'I brought some stuff to trade.'

'Do you really think I'd be interested in these?' He pushed my CD Roms from the counter where I had left them. They fell with a plastic clatter, one of the discs breaking from its sleeve and rolling away across the floor. I made to go and get it.

'Leave it, it's only the Vatican collection. Plenty more where that came from. No my boy, we can strike a bargain here I think. Is that not so, young Ripper? Tell him.'

'Show me the chains again Ted. Put them up for Robbo to see.'

Ted went into his little hut. I could see the top of his head as he moved around, and a picture I hadn't noticed before, a little self-portrait by your man that cut off his ear. It couldn't be real. He came out again and with a grunt, put three objects up onto the counter. A pair of dark boots, like thick-soled Docs, and something that looked like an old fashioned wristwatch.

'Well, Robbo, what do you think?' Ripper was staring at the boots like they were important intergalactic travellers. 'Aren't they *beautiful?*'

They just looked like an old pair of scuffed Docs to me.

'What are you on about?'

'Is it okay, Ted? Can I try them?' Ripper was almost pleading, his face pale and sweaty, like he'd just jacked up.

'Be my guest, skate boy.' The Russian was leaning across the counter, little eyes all dreamy.

Ripper took the Docs, and sat down on a rusty steel chair. He removed his runners, and carefully unzipped the boots. He pulled them onto his feet like they were made of tissue paper, zipped them up, and took a few careful steps. I thought they made him clumsy, a bit more like me. They seemed to be too thick in the soles.

'You'll be needing this.' Ted flipped the watch yoke over to him. Ripper caught it one-handed and velcroed it to his wrist.

'Now Robbo,' he said, 'prepare to be amazed. Watch carefully.'

I did. He touched a control on his wrist and suddenly grew six inches into the air. There was a low sound of metal sliding over metal. I looked real hard. What was going on? Then I had it. The boots had grown a sort of frame from out of their soles, almost like a rollerblade, little ratcheted cogs all inline, and around them, a glistening linked filament like a tiny chain-saw, only without the teeth. He lifted one foot off the floor, and touched the control box again. The room seemed to fill with low music as the chain blurred into movement around the extended superstructure. Chain skates. I had heard about these - got the info from the net - but I'd never believed they were for real. The little chain slowed and stopped. Ripper put the big boot carefully to the floor.

'Watch this.' He pushed himself up from the chair, and set off across the room, skating clumsily, feeling his way. Then, he hit the control, and as the servos driving the chains cut in, allowed himself to be carried by the skates - arms out for balance, but not having to move his feet - in a graceful circle around the room. He got the feel of the skates and started to really go for it, nipping and tucking in among the stacks of gear, spinning and jumping, totally in control, the skates humming like two purring cats. At last, he slid to a halt back at the chair, eyes bright.

'I have to have these Robbo. Don't you see? I have to!' I saw all right. I said. 'But what have you got to trade for them Ripper? They look real expensive.'

'They are. Oh indeed they are. Very very costly.' The little Russian wheezed, arms up on the counter as he rolled a spliff. 'However, our young friend had the foresight to bring certain items with him, and they come some way towards the price.' I hadn't noticed before, but on the counter in front of Ted were several flat slabs of dope - best Clonakilty by the look of it - and a sleek AMCO issue Astra 38 with laser sights. The gear I could understand, but where in the fuck had Ripper got hold of the gun?

Ted prodded the weapon with a long forefinger like he was touching dog shit.

'Reasonable enough merchandise in the normal run of commerce but not quite sufficient to weigh the balance.' He turned his eyes to me, his tongue flicking across his lips. 'However, I am prepared to make a deal.' He lit the spliff with a big metal Zippo, inhaled once, then handed it to me. I took a hit. It seemed like the thing to do.

'Now,' he said, 'to business.'

I don't want to think about how I got home that night. Clutching the big blocks of watercolour paper in under my coat, the paints heavy in the inside pocket, running and stumbling like a Zeroid across the ruined trading estate, heart pounding as I hid from the AMCO patrols.

Searchlights probed the ruins, but they didn't catch me. I moved clumsily from one pool of shadow to the next, trying not to let them hear my frantic breathing. My lung felt like it would burst, the air rattled in it like clinker.

About midnight, the Serenes came in on their bikes, like something from Judge Dredd. Harleys and Yamahas, chromed in the moonlight, engines howling like banshees as they played chicken with the AMCO patrols. I hid, exhausted and scared. Maybe I even fell asleep for a while. When I dared look again, the AMCO boys had fucked off, and the Serenes had lit a fire. I waited, watching them take pot shots at the wild dogs on the edge of the flickering firelight, listening to their crazy slang, shouting to each other across the racket of their boom-boxes. At last they straddled their machines and howled away into the night, allowing me to make my move.

Behind me tracer fire soared into the sky and explosions boomed. The Serenes fighting the Mary Malones, most like, fighting for the right to exist; squabbling like crazed lab-rats, the survivors coupling joylessly out there in the ruins, mindful that tomorrow would be another day.

I don't know what time it was when I got home. I don't know how I got over the compound wall. It was all like a nightmare - one of the ones where you just can't get started at all without something else turning up to delay you - and it's still like a dream to me now.

The main thing was, we all got what we wanted from Big Ted's deal. I got the colours, Ripper had his chain skates, and Big Ted got *all* my drawings, as well as a couple of keys of the best Clon and an interesting sidearm. But I've always thought that I came out of it best - I've still got that box of paints.

Next morning, when Nana woke me with a cup of ersatz, she

almost dropped the tray when she saw what I'd done. She put it down on the bed, and walked slowly to the wall where I had taped up the drawing. I'd made it after I came in, too wound up to sleep. Big Ted, painted from memory, but it was him all right. She'd have known him anywhere. She put her old head to one side, staring at the image.

'Did you do this?' she asked.

'I did.'

'Why?'

'You wouldn't want to know.'

'Did you talk to him?'

'Some.'

She gave me her look, the one that would stop a clock.

'A darling man. Well named. It was time you met.' She touched the drawing with a skittery hand and I thought I saw her blush then, but you couldn't tell with Nana.

She never mentioned Big Ted again, but she set me thinking. Staring at myself in the mirror, and comparing my face with his.

All that was years ago. These days I still do a bit of painting, mostly in oils and egg tempera. That's a tricky one, but it's easier to get hold of and I have learnt to grind a lot of my own colours. The light's about right now, and I have been working on this piece for the last month, trying to catch the feel of the sunset over the harbour. Out here in the west, the light's the thing that interests me now. The sunset over the harbour at Inishbofin. The artist's island.

It took me a while to get here. But I made it in the end. As for the Ripper - I haven't heard of him for years.

I'd say he's still out there.

Carmen Walton

Short-listed in the 1996/97 Fish Short Story Prize

was born in 1961 in Manchester to Scottish parents. It is the tartan-ness of their blood that fires her up at every injustice or irritation. She knows only too well the tough world of art and its brutal rejections. Being told she was too tall to be one of Ken Dodd's Diddy Men, and a little too old, prepared her. Undaunted she pursued her calling. Decades later she finds herself as one half of a Northern England performance poetry duo called *Say So*. Two books of performance poetry, *Something Piggy and Unappealing* and *In a Voice Rich with Irony* have been published. A writer of short stories, television comedy sketches and poetry she explores the unpleasantness of honesty. Recently married after an overlong spell on the shelf, she finds marriage to Ian a lot better than most of her friends said it would be.

White Goods

Carmen Walton

I met him at the art gallery. That gave me the most options. Thing is, if he stood me up in an art gallery no one would know. It could work to my advantage, giving me time to look around, blend in. I was trying to blend in right up to the moment he was due. It was a hot day, over thirty degrees, the signal for all Brits to strip. Flesh met me at every corner.

I was in Post-War Finnish Glass, people watching, considering the legs of everyone who passed me on the way to the Pre-Raphaelite rooms. I love legs; a shapely calf, a chiselled ankle, muscled thighs, male or female. I don't care who they belong to I just appreciate.

'Nettie?'

Disappointment at first sight but I was drifting and didn't bother to say. We shuffled into Urban Landscapes. His hands stuffed into his pockets and his stance let everyone know that this wasn't really his scene. I cast my eye over *Canal 1991, Oil on Canvas* by Jock McFadyen (b. 1950), which let me in. Art has two doors. One says 'piss off', the other 'welcome comrade'. I was at the 'welcome comrade' door for once and I tried to tell him, share the buzz but it went flat. We went and sat in the gallery cafe drinking milky coffee from 1950's repro cups.

Not long after he moved in. Like I said, I was drifting. No priorities or pressing matters to ward him off with. Besides, I fancied a bit of company on the journey downstream.

I neither liked nor disliked him. His nonchalance was interesting. We became in my mind two subjects in a documentary. Gritty. Real life as it is. I monitored my conversations for unseen microphones, watched how I moved in front of hidden cameras. He found my domestic facilities basic and moved his essentials in. The slice of suburbia was at odds with my Spartan set up. For days I didn't touch anything, walked around his belongings weighing them up. Marks and Spencer duvet cover. Sony radio alarm clock. Sharp microwave oven. He had been married. These were his share of the spoils when the marriage had soured. The hidden cameras revealed his other life, moving from black and white to colour.

It didn't take him long to get comfortable. First thing he did was move my tins of Chum and Chappie from the food cupboard to the soap cupboard under the kitchen sink. Said human food and dog food were separate entities. I hadn't seen it like that. Watched daily as rusty rings appeared under the tins in the damp cupboard. Never told him about the dog licks on the plates he ate his food from.

After a few days I accepted the stuff from his other life. Bought two frozen TV dinners to test in the microwave. They made me feel real, like I was in on the game like the people in the adverts. *Prick cellophane with fork. Heat on full for ten minutes. Stir. Heat for a further minute.* I intended to enjoy the lifestyle while it lasted.

There was a pea inside the microwave. It rolled across the revolving base when I opened the door. I slipped it into my pocket away from the razor sharp eyes of the documentary makers. Eating my TV dinner I was careful not to squash the pea. Later, in the bathroom, I held it between my finger and thumb subjecting it to a forensic examination. Before the pea there had been just him and his consumer items. The pea became evidence of a *her*. A previous life where meals were made, served with vegetables. Two people living together, eating food in sauce with peas at the side, each forgetting the take-away meals of their pasts.

The pea was perfect. A pea from a recent meal. What he hadn't told me about his past was whispered to me by the pea. Not many moons and suns had crossed the sky since this had been brought home, in the back of a current reg. hatchback and shoved into a freezer. Where was the freezer now?

I wondered about her. Where was the woman who left her man and a pea from their last portion of peas for me to find? What had happened in the comfort of that life to send them separately, with a collection of white goods, into the world? Somewhere, in a nicer flat than mine, the documentary crew were filming the face of a man who had found a sock, a button, a pubic hair in his new girlfriend's washing machine. This isn't mine, it says all over his face. Twenty screens in the shop front of Dixons show a close up of this man's face saying 'if it isn't mine whose is it?'

We, the surrogate man and I, are in our different bathrooms with items which should be together. Two halves of the same sixpence from a film with a happy ending.

Thin interest in my new man wanes like patterns made by syrup falling from a spoon. He is the intricate design. I am the density of sugar.

'Where does she live now?'

'The estate.'

We do not wrap her in mystery or pretend. There is no jealousy and the pea is hard evidence.

'How do you know?'

Trick question. He won't confess his curiosity. I allow him to get the wrong impression from my line of enquiry.

I am not interested in him. His brooding grief, lovemaking in which I am a vessel disconnected from my soul. I am interested in her. The hidden camera watches my face as I ponder her ability to make decisions and step progressively through her life. I don't

53

want this man, she is saying in the scenario I have invented, he has lost his flavour. I will pay in monthly instalments for a new one. All day I think of her until I begin to wonder what displeased her about him. I have assumed it was she who was displeased.

She isn't difficult to find. Her photograph doesn't capture her exactly but the match is good enough. I am convinced that I would recognise her from her smell which has lingered on the impressive duvet cover which now rests under my nose. Her house on the estate is brand new. A sign on the lawn says 'would visitors be reminded that this house is now occupied'. Everything is recently positioned in this new road, which is too new to be included in the A-Z. In the daytime no one is at home. I pretend I have not seen the warning sign on the lawn and press my nose to the window panes of various rooms to have a close look at her new life. Her kitchen has no awkward corners, overhanging boilers or donated furniture. Cupboards, arranged first on paper by a clever pen, open the same way. There is a space age sheen from the whiteness of her fully fitted electrical appliances. In the corner is a microwave which is like mine but updated. My reflection in her windows tells me that it is hard for me to accept that I have welcomed her used white goods and partner.

'Oy!'

A builder moves me on. Takes a good look at my clothes and his watch in case he needs to give evidence later, when items are reported missing. He too is being filmed for a documentary but won't admit it.

My flat is dull. There is no relationship between the items in the rooms although I felt there was when I chose them. Her man turns my television over with a remote control. His remote control affects me. I have taken her place without being consulted. No matter, I am still drifting and this is company. I would like to be with her in her bright lounge with its oak-effect floors. She could bring coffee to me in surprising cups bought from a little shop tucked away from the masses. She would put thin biscuits, not too many, on a plate for me. I would leave the last one, even though I wanted it.

I understand his loss, although I am not sympathetic. We would both rather be with her.

On Sundays she takes a Scottie dog to the park. Her new man he is never with her. There is no sign on her wedding finger of a discarded ring. The remnants of her life with my man have been folded away with the wedding pictures and pushed out of sight. The Scottie dog is called Rufus. He runs after the sticks she throws, sometimes returning with different ones, bigger than himself. I don't take my eyes off her. If she knows she doesn't show it. The camera watches me through a zoom lens from the cover of bushes. My dog, Patch, looks scruffy next to hers but he is a good dog, a good friend. I would like to walk around the art gallery with her, show her the painting I understood, ask to see her favourite. It is too early to make such suggestions.

One Sunday she sits at the end of the bench and I find the courage to sit at the other. Our dogs have things in common and roll themselves into the same ball to discuss them. We exchange a glance and smile. Dogs! I am prettier than her but her face is smarter. It has considered points of view, made choices, stood by them. She is really alive. I never get beyond thinking. I like her mouth; it turns down at the corners but her lips are full. Two pale segments from which she draws away stray strands of her hair. Hers is a special coat, paid for with what is left after the white goods and new house have been sorted out. We are the same age but she is stronger. She has rejected what I have accepted and moved onto something better.

My attraction towards her becomes complete. I am not a danger to her, she is much stronger than I am. I would like to slip my arm through hers, share a joke that only we can laugh at as we sample perfumes in classy department stores. Her eyes are blue, shaded by lashes and make-up. We don't know each other well enough for her to have rested them openly on mine but I have glimpsed them. I try not to stare and pretend to look at trees in the distance behind her. There are creases by the sides of her lips from where she has laughed and lately cried. My eyes struggle to stay away from her. She has become a subplot in the documentary of my life. I want to slip under her skin; be her for a day. When I go home I will rearrange my furniture, look out for clever prints to personalise my rooms in case she decides to drop by to see me.

Her dog returns to cower away from mine. She digs her hands reassuringly into his short white fur. A pink and pleasing tongue tickles her hand in gratitude. Lucky Rufus is who she loves. Patch lies down in the grass some distance away, pretending he isn't interested. The camera scans us both, pretending not to be interested. Rufus finds his cool again and returns to the fray. He will not be beaten by an underling. She and Rufus are the same. My desire to pierce the membrane surrounding her overwhelms me. I finger the remains of the pea in my pocket and lean forward.

'I have something of yours.' My voice has become a whisper.

'I know,' she replies.

Anne O'Carroll

Runner-up in the 1996/97 Fish Short Story Prize

lives on the Beara Peninsula just a stone's throw from the wild Atlantic Ocean. Indeed she actually spends most of her time throwing stones into it, but also eats chocolate, and does a lot of beachcombing. To fund these deeply satisfying pursuits she works as a journalist, gives training seminars on legal rights, (very seditious), and runs a summer school for foreigners who want to experience Irish culture and improve their English.

Sometimes she writes things.

Flame

Anne O'Carroll

'It'll be a bit like a waxwork,' Mammy had said, 'only it's someone you know.' She was right. When Uncle Tommy lifted him up in his arms so he could see - there lay an exact replica of Uncle Joe. Right down to the smile crinkles around his eyes, and the quirky little grin. Only the fingernails weren't right - a kind of bluish white instead of the proper pearly pink. It made him feel a bit funny to look at them.

Everyone in the room was dressed as if they were at a party. Even Uncle Tommy had a tie on, and a jacket. The tie was soft and silky like Frank's blankie, and the jacket was made of some rough stuff that tickled his face when Uncle Tommy lifted him up and held him tight. But it didn't feel like a proper party. Nobody was holding a drink, and there were no little bowls of peanuts. Everyone looked sad and streaky, and clustered in little groups, talking in low voices. While they talked, their eyes kept straying back to the waxwork of Uncle Joe.

If he'd only been there Uncle Joe would have explained everything in a jiffy. He was brilliant like that. When other grown-ups scorned you or got complicated, Uncle Joe just lifted the lid off the mystery, as clear as anything. Frank had been afraid of thunder until Uncle Joe explained it. Elaine had laughed and teased and poked fun when thunder rattled the rafters and Frank cowered in terror under the duvet. He had wanted to scream and slap her and poke her in the eye, but she was two years older and would surely tell. Instead he had wet himself and Mammy had been cross even though she smiled and said not to worry.

But now he was in the know, and Elaine's mockery was thwarted. 'Ah sure, thunder is easy explained,' Uncle Joe had revealed. 'Ye see, every now and then all the angels up in heaven have a go on their roller skates, and God makes them take up the carpet so they don't ruin it. But underneath the carpet is only bare floorboards, so the wheels of the skates make an awful racket - and that's thunder!'

From then on, snug in his bed, in the belly of the storm, Frank was entranced by his mind's eye image of huge angels in Doc Marten roller skates, careering wildly up and down the vast wooden corridors of heaven. Limbs akimbo, white robes hoiked up over their hairy shins, they wildly flapped mammoth wings to keep their balance. He had figured out all on his own that it was the beating of wings that made the wind. Captivated by these enormous frolicking friendly beings, he lay in bed contentedly sucking his thumb and refusing to talk to Elaine. For some reason, she now was the one who went into Mammy and Daddy's room during storms.

Now Elaine was standing at the other side of the big box, looking with interest at Uncle Joe's waxwork and its funny fingernails. Mammy stood close behind with her hands on Elaine's shoulders. She bent over and quietly spoke to her. As the words trickled into the child's ear the expression of curiosity in her eyes gradually changed - shifted into something unfathomable.

'Doesn't he look nice?' murmured Uncle Tommy in Frank's ear. 'Who?' asked Frank. 'Your Uncle Joe,' replied Tommy with a slight nod at the big box.

Frank stared. Everyone in the room suddenly fell away and

there was only him and Uncle Tommy and the box, all balancing on the head of a pin. Frank held his breath and clung tighter in case they fell off. A funny feeling jolted through his body, like the time he had touched the electric fence at Grandad's.

Uncle Tommy gently rubbed his back and said 'Hmmmm? and gradually the people and the sound of talking slowly surged back around them. Frank let out his breath with a gasp. 'I thought it was a waxwork,' he whispered, mortified.

'I wish to God it was,' said Uncle Tommy in a chokey voice and when Frank looked at his face he saw to his amazement that his cheeks were slick with wetness and big drops were falling from his chin.

It hadn't always been like this. Uncle Joe and Uncle Tommy were Frank's favourite relatives on account of being the funniest. They were always having a laugh. Uncle Tommy was from Donegal and so Uncle Joe - a midlands man - was always slagging him, saying things like 'Don't mind that aul' mountainy man.' Uncle Tommy would invariably reply, 'Sure what would you know you aul' bog trotter, ye.' But it was all in fun. They were really the best of friends. And they were special too, because of Uncle Joe being Frank's godfather. He had one up on Elaine with that, because her godfather lived in America and almost never sent her presents on her birthday or anything.

Once Frank had asked Uncle Joe, 'If you're my godfather, what's Uncle Tommy then?' They had been doing the washing up, while Frank did his jigsaw puzzle of Thomas the Train on the kitchen table. There was a short, uncustomary silence, and Frank looked up from his puzzle. Both men were looking at each other in a funny stuck sort of way. Uncle Joe held a plate, from which the suds dripped like sloppy lace. Uncle Tommy had a blue bowl in one hand - the dishcloth dangled damply from the other.

Joe turned and quietly asked, 'What do you mean, Frank?' Frank suddenly felt flustered. 'Well,' he ventured uncertainly,

'Uncle Sean is my uncle because he's married to mammy's sister Aunty Margaret, and you're Daddy's brother... so...' He petered off, feeling muddled. 'Oh, it's simple so,' cried Uncle Tommy, suddenly brisk and bright. 'If Joe is your godfather, then that must make me your fairy godmother!' He turned the bowl upside down on his head, flapped the dishcloth and did a dainty pirouette with such a daft expression on his face that Frank laughed delightedly and spilled a load of jigsaw pieces on the floor.

Scrabbling under the table for them he glanced up and saw Uncle Joe shoot an uncustomarily cross look at Uncle Tommy, before carrying on with the washing up, loudly clunking the sudsy dishes down on the draining board. Tommy raised his eyebrows, shrugged and started hanging the dried cups on the dresser. Frank wondered if Uncle Joe was a bit cross because he hadn't understood the question. Or maybe he was a bit jealous of Uncle Tommy getting to show off for a change. But then he found the two pieces that completed the engine's chimney and forgot all about it.

Frank looked up at Uncle Tommy's face with concern. The tears that fell on his jacket soaked into the rough tweed without leaving a trace, but the drops that fell on his silky blue tie made navy spots come up on it. Frank rubbed one with his finger but it didn't come off. He put his mouth up to Uncle Tommy's ear and whispered urgently, 'Your tie is getting spotty.'

'Good lad, good boy yourself. Sure, come on and we'll clean it up,' said Tommy and sat down on an empty chair, settling Frank on his knee. He took out a handkerchief, wiped his face, blew his nose and inhaled deeply in great shuddering breaths. Frank wiped at the tie with a tissue but the spots didn't soak off. Little bits of tissue just wrinkled off and stuck to it. Noticing his forlorn look Tommy said, 'Don't worry, pet. It'll be grand. Sure, it'll dry out. Let's just sit here for a moment, the pair of us.'

They sat and looked around them. Frank could still see Uncle

Joe's face, lying quietly at the top of the box, and his hands folded on his tummy. Throngs and throngs of people were coming in and filing past. There was a whole group of younger grown-ups with pink puffy eyes who arrived in a group. They came up to Uncle Tommy. Each one kissed and hugged him, took him by the hand, looked him in the eyes saying 'Oh Tommy, I'm sorry, I'm so sorry.'

Then they went to the box, and looked down hungry-eyed at Uncle Joe. Several of them said something to him as they passed, but so low that Frank couldn't hear it. Others didn't say anything, but stared so intently and with such a strange look that Frank was sure they were speaking directly to him. 'Can he hear them?' he asked Uncle Tommy, nodding at the group around the box. 'Of course he can. He'll be able to hear us all of the time now, Frankie,' he replied.

Uncle Joe was the best listener of all the grown-ups he knew. Whenever he told stories you just *knew* he'd been listening to you because he brought into the story all the things you had told him that day, but made them so magical and different that you all of a sudden realised that the hero of the story was really you. The most magical stories were actually true ones: the ones about science. The absolute best was the real, true story of fire. One night when he and Elaine were staying over while Mammy and Daddy went to the theatre, he had snuck down to the sitting room after she fell asleep. They were sitting on the sofa in front of the fire reading newspapers, and both looked up smiling when he came in. 'I can't sleep,' he said sheepishly.

'Of course you can't. Sure it's criminal the way they send kids to bed so early nowadays,' said Tommy sympathetically from behind his newspaper. Frank crawled up onto the sofa between them and sat for a while in companionable silence. Sandwiched between the sheets of crackling newspapers he felt like a little rowing boat between two ships in full sail. He fixed his eyes on the leaping coal flames and fired a shot across their bows: 'Where do flames come from?' he asked nonchalantly.

When he was at home he would collect interesting questions to ask the Uncles. They always had great answers, and Joe had once told him he was sure to become a famous scientist if he kept on asking such interesting questions. He knew the drill at this stage. If you could ask a good question you got to stay up later, because they loved to answer them so much that they wouldn't send you back to bed until they were quite sure you completely understood the answer. Every time he asked the question with just the right mixture of curiosity and casualness. Curiosity so they'd think it had just occurred to him. And casual so they'd know that he half knew the answer already, and wouldn't really be upset if they couldn't come up with the explanation. But they had never let him down.

Usually there was a little silence after the question. He knew by now that the longer the silence, the better the reply, so he waited with baited breath, sneaking a sidelong look at Uncle Joe's profile. 'Well now...' said Uncle Joe folding up his newspaper and laying it down beside the sofa, 'Where do flames come from...? Sit up here on my knee till I tell ye.' Frank scrambled eagerly up onto his lap and snuggled down, his eyes locked on the flickering fire.

'Let's see now,' said Uncle Joe, 'long, long ago when the world was young and big knobbly dinosaurs used to trundle through Dublin looking for stray dogs to eat, the whole earth was covered in forest. And these forests were huge. They had big trees as big as Liberty Hall, with leaves as big as Morris Minors and all those trees used to do all day long is soak up the sun from the sky and slurp up the water through their roots, and sway in the wind and sing away happily to themselves.

'The vegetarian dinosaurs - the ones who didn't eat stray dogs - used to munch at the lower leaves of these trees, but they couldn't reach the top ones because they were so big. And so the trees grew and grew and when they got old and couldn't think of any more songs to sing they keeled over and settled down into the mud and started to turn back into earth.'

'But what's that got to do with flames?' asked Frank.

'Patience now, young fella,' said Uncle Joe. 'I'm getting to it. Well, as I was saying, the big, huge, giant trees and all the smaller plants eventually died and snuggled down into the mud to turn back into the earth, but then it started to rain. And it rained and rained and rained and there was such a huge flood in all the low places (*Noah*... breathed Frank) 'that the poor auld trees couldn't get enough oxygen to turn properly back into soil.'

'What's oxygen?' asked Frank. 'It's a very, very pure kind of air, the same way whiskey is a very pure kind of water,' explained Tommy. 'Tommy,' said Uncle Joe, mock stern, 'who's telling this story...?' 'Fine so,' said Uncle Tommy in a mock offended voice and winked at Frank before disappearing behind his newspaper again.

'Anyway, as I was saying,' said Uncle Joe, 'the poor auld trees just lay there in the wet and couldn't turn back into earth. So they decided to turn into something new instead. And the ground folded and folded and squashed them up - like your mammy does with the dough when she's making bread - and they got squashed up until they went really hard and black, and formed big lines of this black stuff in the ground like stony snakes.'

He paused and took a drink from his cup of tea. Frank contemplated the snakes: dark, still and beady-eyed, down in the deep. 'So then one day, hundreds and thousands and millions of years later, some baldy little pink animals took over the earth. Ye see, the dinosaurs had all been killed off by the flu which they'd caught after the downpour, and these creatures were distant relatives of the stray dogs from way back. Anyway, they were miserable little things and had no fur of their own so they were always catching chills and colds and coughing and sneezing. And they had no Lemsip or anything that time so they were always shivering and olagoning and complaining.

'Now, to take their minds off their frostbite and chilblains and sniffles these fellas had wonderful storytellers. They had all the history of the world in their heads and they would sit around and tell of the times way back when dinosaurs stalked the land and the sun shone every day and all the trees had to do was sit and soak up the lovely heat and light and sing in the wind. And they told about the floods and the squashed up trees that couldn't turn back into earth, and one day one smart young wee fella - about your age - he was listening to the story and he had an idea. He was a bit of a bright spark really, always asking questions, and he just jumped up and cried out, "But if the trees soaked up all that sunshine over the hundreds of years then all those hot summers must still be there, trapped inside."

'Well, it seemed like a bit of a tall tale at the time, and he was very wee, so I'm afraid to say that his big sister and some of her friends just laughed at him, but the wise old woman of the tribe sat and sucked her pipe and said, "Whisht yer laughing. How do you know that isn't true till you try it out." So the whole tribe got up and went off and got their buckets and spades and dug up some of the old black knobbly bits of thousand year old trees and put them in a pile and everyone sat around looking at them. But they were just black and dusty and they lay there and didn't do anything at all. So everybody laughed at him and went off on to hunt for frogs to make some nice slimy frog pie for the tea.' ('Yech,' said Frank with feeling.)

'Well the wee fella (his name was Furg) was very disappointed at his failure. He had a sort of an idea that he might have been able to squeeze the stored up hot summers out of the old tree remains and save the tribe from the never-ending misery of cold toes and shivery sniffles. But he was a feisty little fella, so he didn't give up. He went to the nearest bushes and broke off two old dry sticks that were lying on the ground, and he sharpened them into two points. And using the two points he gouged away at the black stuff like mad, trying to split them open and see if the lovely golden glow of hot summer days would spill out like the yolk out of an egg.

'But he had no luck. He was just about to give up when a little bird which had been sitting on a nearby bush watching him flew down and landed on his shoulder. "You silly ninny," said the bird, "that's not how you do it. You have to rub the two sticks together and then when the magic starts to happen feed it dry leaves and more twigs and *then,* put the stony snakes on top and they'll give you back your summer."

'Well, Furg got such a shock that that's just what he did. He rubbed the two dry sticks together until they got hotter and hotter, and suddenly smoke started to come out of them. Then he covered them up with dry leaves, and *they* started to smoke. The little bird fanned them with her wings and suddenly Furg saw a new little red leaf spring up among the brown dried ones. But this leaf was alive and it wavered and danced in the breeze. When he added more twigs, more little red and orange and yellow leaves grew, and then, when he put the black stones on top they started to crackle and spit and turn orange and a lovely heat came out of them and warmed his knees and the smoke turned from grey to black and all the tribe came running up to see what was going on.

'When they saw what was happening, they lifted up Furg on their shoulders and danced around and had a big party for three days and three nights, and there was a special holiday from school. Everyone went mad collecting the bits of black stony snakes and even made tunnels down into the ground to get at them. The whole tribe was toasty warm and comfortable and made Furg their king, because he was so clever and had the wit to ask good questions and not give up when people laughed at him. Furg was a good and merry king and lived to be 103. In fact in the history books he's still known as Old King Coal, to this very day.'

Frank stared in fascination at the glowing coal fire, its shimmering waves of golden heat, the hot pulsing embers. 'Wow,' he breathed. The room was quiet except for the gentle snoring of the dog, slumbering in oblivion in front of the fire. Uncle Tommy too, had put down his paper and was gazing at the fire. 'Is that really, really true?' asked Frank. 'Yep,' said Uncle Joe. 'What you're looking at there is the concentrated summers of millions of years ago.'

'What's turf so?' asked Frank.

'It's the same with turf only turf is younger so it's just the summers from hundreds and thousands of years ago,' explained Joe. 'And if we burned the wood of a tree that was in Grandad's garden when he was a lad, we'd be warming our knees on the summers that Grandad had when he was a boy. Imagine!'

'Wow,' said Frank, utterly bowled over. 'Wow.' He stared, mesmerised at the tongues of flame, curving and flickering. Slithery dinosaurs and snakes darted their heads out at him and disappeared back into the glow. The burning mound of coal slowly shifted, gracefully collapsed in on itself coalescing into glowing embers. Time started to telescope and when sleep claimed him, warm strong arms gathered him up and carried his limp, slumbering body up to bed.

Frank snuggled closer in to Tommy's chest. Mammy and Elaine were over with the cousins, but he felt safe with his big arms around him, as if he blended into the tweed jacket like a chameleon, and no one could see him at all. There were old people coming in now. Old grandfather men in caps and dark suits who looked awkward and ill at ease until Frank's grandparents came forward to greet them. One of the old men stood awhile at the top of the box gazing at Uncle Joe with tired watery blue eyes. In one swift move he swooped down and kissed him on the forehead, tenderly laid a gnarled hand on his cheek and walked quickly away swiping at his cheeks with the back of his hand.

'Are we allowed to touch him?' asked Frank in amazement.

'We are indeed,' said Uncle Tommy and carried him over to the box. The two stood looking down at the young man lying in the coffin. Uncle Tommy reached out his free hand and tenderly smoothed down the fluffy brown hair against Joe's marble white forehead.

'I want to give him a kiss,' whispered Frank in his ear. He jerkily nodded his assent and held Frank tight so the boy could lean out over the box. The child solemnly kissed the pale cheek. It felt cool and firm against his warm, soft lips, like the soft cool leather of the sofa at home. He patted Uncle Joe's hair with his soft pudgy hand and gave him a sweet conspiratorial smile. Turning back to Uncle Tommy a huge weariness washed over him. 'I'm tired,' he said.

'Good boy,' said Uncle Tommy, 'you're grand. Your Mammy'll take you home now.'

Later, at home in bed he asked her what happened to him. She was sitting on the edge of the bed stroking his forehead. Daddy was in saying goodnight to Elaine. 'Bad things started to grow in his tummy,' she said sadly, 'and they hurt him and in the end they stopped him from living. It was very sudden, nobody expected it.'

'But couldn't God send him any medicine to make him better?'

'No. God wanted him to come up and help him look after the angels with him.'

'So he really is completely dead?'

'Yes.'

There was a short pause. His Mammy was looking at the night light, her eyelashes long and sweeping on her shadowed profile. 'Will he still be dead tomorrow?' he asked hopefully.

'I'm afraid so, lovey,' she replied turning her luminous eyes towards him.

Frank was silent for a while. His mother looked at him with pain in her eyes, her cool long-fingered hand stroking the child's forehead. 'Let's say our prayers now and we'll pray for Uncle Joe too.'

Frank folded his hands and bowed his head. 'Now I lay me down to sleep, I pray the Lord my soul to keep, If I... if I should...' He stuttered to a halt - a hard cold marble in his throat and a desperate rushing roar in his ears. 'If I should...'

Suddenly his mammy's arms were around him, she was holding him tight, rocking him forward and back, forward and back, pressing him close to her soft warm, mammy-smelling front. 'It's alright pet, it's alright.' She was crying and he was crying and everything was a jumble of wet salt, soft warm arms, flannel pyjama collars and wet strands of hair. 'It's alright pet, it's alright. It's OK,' she said more calmly rocking him gently. 'We'll all die sometime, but usually it won't be for years and years and years, until we're really old, much older than Uncle Joe.'

Frank digested this, stuffing Teddy under his oxter. He wanted to ask why it was in the prayer so, but he couldn't. It rattled and echoed in his head, and he couldn't shake it out - 'If I should die before I wake, I pray the Lord my soul to take, if I should die before I wake, if I should die before I wake...' A huge wave of languorous tiredness swept over him, threatened to swamp him entirely. But suddenly a bright thought, an easier one to grab a hold of, bobbed up like an orange buoy.

'Uncle Tommy said I could have one of Heidi's puppies when they're born. He said Uncle Joe wanted me to have one.'

'That's great news,' said Mammy, with a breathy little laugh.

'We'll have to go over and see Uncle Tommy to get the puppy,' said Frank. 'We'll still be visiting Uncle Tommy won't we Mammy? I mean he has to show me how to train the little puppy and everything.' After a brief pause his Mammy said, 'Of course we will sweetie, of course we will.' She tucked him in tight and gave him a long squeeze and a kiss. 'Go to sleep now, pet. We've all had a long day.'

He watched the flame of the nightlight flicker, heard the creak of his mother's footsteps down the stairs; the low rumble of his father's voice and his mother's muffled wavering reply. The shadows danced on the wall like silk scarves on a clothesline. His eyelids started to droop. Nothing really made any sense, and he felt really, really tired just trying to think about it all. There seemed to be a small cold stone stuck in the middle of his chest.

'G'night,' he said to the flame of the nightlight. He humped up his body into a tightly curled ball, and wearily let his eyes close. Teddy's nose dug snugly into his armpit. With a small sigh he cast off - out, out into the steep, into the deep, into the dark, swirling small death of sleep - helplessly, trustingly adrift between the daylight-lit love of his family and the guiding lighthouse glow of his Uncle Joe on the far, far, distant shore.

In memoriam, J.M.

Frank O'Donovan

Runner-up in the 1996/97 Fish Short Story Prize

Lives in County Cork with his wife, family and tolerant in-laws. He is currently building a new house and everybody who buys this book is invited to the house-warming. He describes his own looks as 'stunning' but a local garda has gone on record as saying that he 'looks like a gouger'. Frank has visited a number of prisons in recent months and has had difficulty getting out for this reason.

He started his day job as a journalist with *The Sunday World,* breaking a number of hugely influential stories the subject matter of which escapes him at present, and his career went uphill from there. He now works as an ace reporter with *The Southern Star.* Before that he studied at UCC and lived in Italy for a time, leaving in a huff when he failed to get deported. An unpaid subway fine is still on record with the Italian police.

His literary influences include Gunther Grass, Gabriel Garcia Marquez, Graham Greene, Naomi Campbell.

Johnny Mok's Universe

Frank O'Donovan

Dodie was here again this morning. Here in the room. The minute I woke up he was sitting in the chair near the door, looking at me with that habitual smirk on his face, his nose turned up and his eyes sparkling in his head. He's been here constantly with me for the past few months. Every day. I'm getting really sick of him and I wish he'd fuck off.

But I suppose I have only myself to blame. After all, it's my fault that he's here. I brought him here, in a manner of speaking, but the chain of events that led to him sitting there staring at me like a half-wit was set in motion a long time ago. It led to me being here, and me bringing him along with me. Making him manifest, I think is what the doctor called it.

And, to be honest, there are times when I like having him here. Especially on bad winter nights when I feel alone and isolated in this room. It's OK too when there's a storm and the lights flicker on and off, occasionally plunging the room into darkness, in this long grey building of pinnacles and towers. I don't mind because Johnny Mok prepared me for all that years ago. I even feel comforted by the sound of wailing and shouting from down the corridors, like the way you feel comforted by the sound of distant dogs barking in the night when you are tucked up in bed.

Years ago my Ma told me to keep away from Johnny Mok

because he had spent most of his life in Our Lady's lunatic asylum. 'What are you sitting around at night with him for? You should be in doing your homework, not walloping around the streets with that madman.' My granny, her mother, was dying in the back room of our house at the time. This was making her edgy so I let the comments about Johnny Mok go.

Anyway, I knew that Johnny Mok had spent a lot of time in Our Lady's, the longest building in Cork. Grey blocks with turrets and pinnacles and countless windows. Johnny told me the loonies went ape on stormy nights when lightning crackled and thunder shook the building. There was mayhem if the lights went out. I imagined Johnny Mok sitting behind one of those windows, sitting up in bed like he did for twelve months.

He told me about it the night I told him Granny was dying, after Dodie had loped off in the rain to hang around the side of Hogan's shop. He fasted for six months in Our Lady's and for a full twelve months he sat up in bed all night. 'There's no knowing what I have suffered,' he said. Now that he was out of the turrets and pinnacles he had no intention of going back. The doctor with the red car often called to Johnny Mok's poky house on the edge of our estate and tried to get him back into Our Lady's. But he wouldn't go because he said he didn't want to go back into any institution.

One evening after the doctor had left in disgust Johnny Mok brought me into his house for the first time. It was filthy and all his possessions were wrapped in newspaper, as if he was going to put them into storage. His old black and white tv set was the only unwrapped item. 'Are you going somewhere?' I asked.

'Where would I be going at me age, kiddo?'

'With the doctor, back to...'

'Look, no way am I ever going back there. And he can't make me, he has nothing to pin on me. I told him there's only one doctor for me now and that's the doctor who made the world.'

Granny was dying in the back room of our house, with the lighted candles going all day and the black crucifix and all, but Johnny Mok told me he had the whole thing about death worked out. He put it into perspective for me the night I told him about her, leaning against the jamb of his open front door.

'She'll die in one bed and wake up in another one. Why be afraid of dying? It's like going from Cork to Limerick,' he said.

Darkness was beginning to fall and the rain that had poured all day continued to come down in sheets, sloping against the wall of the house. Johnny Mok gathered his tattered raincoat tightly around him. Dodie sat on the railing outside the house, oblivious to the drenching he was getting. He remembered bible stories from school about people coming back from the dead.

'What about Lazarus? Did he really become a man again?' he said.

'Ah, that's a mystery,' said Johnny Mok.

'But there must have been a pong offa him, he was dead for four days.'

'But what's four days in eternity, kiddo?'

Johnny Mok was regarded as a religious freak, but he was no bigot. Every Sunday he went to the 11 o'clock Protestant service in Shandon and from there went to 12 o'clock Mass in the North Cathedral. He wrote comments about the sermons in both churches, writing furiously in a back seat in his neat, spidery handwriting, and then stuck them onto the notice boards. He dressed in white for the annual Corpus Christi procession, walking through Patrick St in front of Bishop Lucey who held the monstrance under a canopy.

When he moved to the estate in the late 1960s his long black hair and penetrating stare made him a dead ringer for Charles Manson who was hitting the headlines at the time, after the Tate murder. The estate was made up of mainly young couples back then and the fear he inspired fuelled his isolation and made him a loner. I felt sorry for him because I believed his isolation had made him eccentric but Ma told me he was a loony from day one.

In his seventies his straggly hair was grey and an unruly stubble replaced the luxurious beard that had once been mocked around the estate.

Dodie was two years older than me. When I was a kid he seemed like an ogre out of a storybook, running wild around the estate. When we were growing up he stood head and shoulders over the other kids so it was natural that they would look up to him in fear. By the time of Granny's death he was nearly eighteen and had built up a formidable rep as a hard man. He kept his head shaved all year and his prominent two front teeth and turned up nose gave him an almost comical look when he smiled, like the guy out of the Mad comic strip. But anyone who knew him would not have taken him for a figure of fun. And if they did they paid the price, goodo. Even relatives weren't safe as his cousin Derry Martin, who Dodie stabbed with a scissors outside a chipper, found out.

Granny died in her sleep and Johnny Mok said he would get in touch with her on his screen. He was in touch with everybody in the universe through his screen, he told me. I met him on the green outside his house a few nights after the funeral. He brought me into the house and showed me his old, battered tv set.

'This is my line to them all. All I have to do is call them up on the screen, like the Lord,' he said.

'Can you talk to Granny? Do you know where she is?' He looked at me but his mind seemed a universe away.

'She's with God, so she's happy.'

'How do you know she isn't in hell?' I said, remembering the Christian Brothers' accounts of sinners thrown into the eternal fires.

'Look, God the Father is no relation to us at all. It wouldn't do for him to throw everybody down to hell. But God the Son, he was different. He had a temper alright. Look at when he threw that crowd out of the temple. He was just like you and me.'

'But my Ma says Granny was a sinner, that we're all sinners.'

'Kiddo, there's no sin, no sin at all. Priests and popes, the whole lot will be treated the same, heads of state, the lot. There will be penance for a time but then we will all get these lovely castles and all, we'll all be friends and we'll go to dances. I have it first hand. Your Granny will get back her prime again. She wasn't afraid of dying, why would she be?'

'It's like going from Cork to Limerick,' he said as he gave a black-toothed grin.

I told Dodie about Johnny's screen that night. He called me over as I was on my way home after visiting Johnny. He was sitting at a bonnah, with a few others, on a patch of waste ground at the end of a terrace of houses. He motioned me to sit, handed me a butt which I choked on.

'Why were you up in that old fucker's house?' he said.

'How did you know where I was?'

'I seen ya. I keeps a watch on ya, boy,' he said, waving his hands menacingly in my face as the others sniggered.

I was still afraid of this violent and unpredictable fiend and I felt a knot tightening in my stomach. The others sitting around, for all their bravado, were scared as well. Dodie seemed to have a special centre of gravity and the rest of us in the circle were pulled towards him, dragged down by the irresistible force of his aggression. I told him about the screen, and the words were out of my mouth before my brain got a handle on the situation. Dodie's attention was focused immediately. 'So, he talks to stiffs on the screen?'

The others shifted and suppressed sniggers.

'He's a mad bastard,' said Larry Murphy, tapping the side of his head with his index finger.

'Shut yer hole, who the fuck asked you anything?' I shouted.

Dodie laughed at him. 'Down boy, get back in yer fuckin' box and stay there,' he said.

I remembered the expression of defiance and pride on Larry's face, months earlier, as he was led away from Cork courthouse to serve a seven day sentence for contempt. An assault charge against Dodie was struck out when the victim baulked at giving evidence at the last minute. Larry had threatened, at the back of the courthouse, to kick the guy's head in again if he grassed on Dodie. The guy had no option but to pull out of giving evidence. Larry was caught making the threat by a garda and got seven days, which added to his rep and, he hoped, his status in the eyes of Dodie.

Triumphant in the local pub that night Dodie warned anybody within earshot what would happen to those who grassed on him or any other member of the gang, and the word spread from there.

Dodie turned away from Larry's sheepish look and fixed his steady gaze on me. 'D'ye think he'd show me this screen if I go up to him?' he said.

The first thing I became aware of was the vague blue flashing on the wall of my bedroom. The light came through a crack in the curtains and its intermittent flashing must have woken me up. When I heard the racket on the street I wondered why I hadn't woken up sooner. The blue lights of ambulance and patrol cars swept over the front of Johnny Mok's house at different and disconcerting angles, making me feel dizzy. The crowd, with coats over their night clothes, pushed forward with a sigh as Johnny Mok was wheeled from the house and placed in the back of an ambulance. I tried to push through the crowd to reach him but he was enclosed in the back before I got out. The gardai dispersed the crowd and one garda was left at the gate of Johnny's house so there was nothing I could do but go home and wait for news.

It was five am when I got back to my bedroom but I was too

raw and wide awake with adrenalined energy to go back to sleep. I looked out of the window at the dawn that was just beginning to crack open the horizon and strained to get a glimpse of Johnny's house through my window. It looked cold and wet, draped in shadows in the grey pre-dawn light.

I remembered Johnny telling me that he never wanted to go back to an institution. He was lucky, if that's the word, that he never regained consciousness in the North Infirmary hospital where he died from head injuries three days after the attack. I heard it on the 6.30 news that morning: an elderly man, beaten in the course of a robbery when he surprised the culprit. It was believed that the culprit got away with a few hundred pounds in cash and an old black and white tv set. The gardai were investigating but had little to go on. The tv was found in a skip a week later.

The word on the street filled in the blanks. The gardai pulled in a few suspects, Dodie among them, but whoever did it left no traces. There were no fingerprints and nobody knew anything that they were prepared to talk about. There was no evidence to pin it on anybody. But I knew it was Dodie who had broken one of the glass panels on Johnny Mok's back door, looking for the black handbag where Johnny put the money he collected for his pension every week. He had poked around the flat the night I had brought him to see Johnny's screen, pretending interest and wonder as Johnny explained the ins and outs of his magic gift. 'It's all clear to me now,' he said to me, winking, as we left the house.

The night of the attack I had seen him heading home, tanked up on drink and dope, around one am. I didn't see him for a few days and he was taken in for questioning the day Johnny died, to be released within hours for want of evidence. For weeks afterwards I saw him swanning around the streets, drinking and smoking around the bonnah at night with the rest of the gang, at ease in the tight circle of his influence.

The burden of guilt didn't seem to weigh on Dodie too much, but it was sure getting up my nose. The warning about grassing and his formidable rep remained at the front of my mind but another image lurked there too: of Johnny Mok laid out in his coffin in the mortuary of the hospital, irregular black stitching holding the skin of his forehead together where Dodie had hit him repeatedly with what the gardai had called a blunt instrument. He looked sad and abandoned, as if he knew somehow that his death would go unpunished. I was shocked when I saw him, I thought a man with his belief in the certainty of an afterlife would look as peaceful as Granny had.

The rain stopped as I came out from under the tree where I had been sheltering in Currykippane Cemetery. Dark clouds parted to show a deep, cobalt blue sky and stars that were slightly obscured by the glare of the city lights. Currykippane was the highest graveyard in the city, overlooking a night vista made up of endless strings of orange street lights. I was waiting with my heart in my mouth for Mick Mullins, the only guy from our estate to become a garda.

He would have been disowned for sleeping with the enemy only for his easy-going manner. If he was trying to collar a guy or get information out of him he went the long way about it, drawling out words in his gravelly voice, offering a cigarette, non-threatening, not even looking at him until he had him where he wanted him. Two months after Johnny Mok's death I phoned Mick from a phone box in the city at three am.

'Mick, it's me. I need to talk to you.'

'Wha'defuck? Who's 'at ringing at this time of the night?' he said in a voice thick with sleep and cigarettes.

'It's me. Y'know, me, an' it's urgent. I need to see you.' The voice finally clicked with him and he heard enough to realise it was important.

'See ya tomorrow night in de Curra,' he signed off, rolling over in the bed before he hung up the phone.

The next morning, at two am, he came through the squeaky gate of Currykippane, the red tip of a cigarette glowing between his teeth and we had our secret rendezvous under the stars.

'Jeez, do you ever sleep,' he said, giving me a playful dig in the arm.

'Not much lately, no,' I replied. He threw the cigarette on the wet grass and stepped on it. Shitting bricks, I blurted what I knew in a hoarse whisper I was convinced could be heard all over the city. Burly Mick looked like he could take on Dodie and whatever army would back him, but he must have heard my knees knocking.

'Don't worry,' he said, waving an arm over the rows of headstones. 'Nobody here will take a blind bit o' notice.'

'Tisn't the dead I'm worried about.'

Like in the movies Mick promised never to reveal his source. Dodie was hauled off to the Bridewell the day after the graveyard get-together and played a game of nerves with Mick. Mick sat opposite Dodie, offered him a cigarette and asked about his father. Dodie relaxed as Mick continued in the same vein, talking about his family, soccer, the weather and the merits of the film *Robocop*. After an hour he dropped the bomb: he had an eyewitness, prepared to testify that he had seen Dodie coming out of Johnny Mok's back window with a tv set on the night of the murder. Dodie cracked and made a statement, admitting it all. Mick, who had played cards with Dodie on street corners and even shared a school bench with him for a week, had no problem with Dodie's one stab at keeping his rep intact: the word went out on the street that Mick had bet the confession out of him.

I carried Dodie around in my head for years. He was there in my head during his ten years in prison and afterwards when he went to England. And even after I got depressed and ended up in my little room here, which for all I know is the very room Johnny

81

Mok had sat upright in for twelve months, he was with me.

But then, as the good old doc with the squint tells me, I made him manifest and the fucker came out of my head and took to sitting on the chair near the door, as if we were the best of buddies, smirking at me. But I don't care anymore because I know it will all be over soon: this afternoon I heard the news that Dodie had died in England, stabbed during a fight. I felt an instant relief and buried my head in my hands. When I dared to look up again the chair by the door was empty. I felt no emotion at the news of his death, just relief that the nightmare was over at last.

Julia Darling

Runner-up in the 1996/97 Fish Short Story Prize

lives in Newcastle upon Tyne. She has been writing stories for some time, and her collection *Bloodlines* was published by Panurge Press. She has had several stories on the radio, and has recently completed a commissioned play *Eating The Elephant*. She also writes and performs with *The Poetry Virgins*.

Three Stages Of Heat

Julia Darling

Tepidarium.

Just after Mel died the boiler broke. The pilot light went out.

It hung on the wall, lifelessly, its wires gaping. It was the coldest November there had ever been. I phoned up. The gas board put me on hold and played a violin sonata.

Later a man came smelling of nylon and solder. He said the boiler needed a part from France; he drew me a picture. It looked just like a drawing pin to me. It could take at least a month, he said. The man had a pipe-shaped mouth.

He took his bag of impotent tools and limped off, leaving me standing dressed in three cardigans in the hallway.

I bought an electric heater, but I've always found that electricity gives me a rash, so I started to wander around the city, in the way that crazy people do; just sitting in a cafe wearing too many clothes, or sifting through strange objects in department stores, (amazing how they let you do that when you're obviously not going to buy anything), or listening to broken street musicians and screaming evangelists. I gawped into the windows of offices and was drawn to gouged-out buildings where groups of workmen hung around flickering braziers, holding red hands over the flames. I wanted to join them, but walked on. They didn't see me as I plodded past in my damp and flaccid shoes. Shivering.

People probably thought I was on day release from some kind of institution. In fact I once worked for the gas board. You might have thought I had some connections, boiler wise, but I didn't. I was one of the old Bunsen school. These days it's all automatic. Parts from Europe. Showrooms full of appliances wrapped in plastic bags.

Mel had a smoky sense of humour. She used to tease me about the way I picked the bits of fluff up from the carpet in desperate lunges. I can't have been that bad. We lived together for nearly fourteen years. We met at the gas board. She worked in cookers, and I was in central heating. Fell in love. After that it was just me and her. Eating vegetarian goulash together around the kitchen table.

Playing Ladies Bowls.

Me cutting the grass, her putting it into black plastic bags.

The funeral was pleasant enough. Some of the women came from the cooker department. There was Mel's sister and most of the lesbian ladies bowling team. We'd not seen many people towards the end. Mel's illness was a quiet and beautiful time. Misty, careful. Her decay reminded me of a fire slowly going out. In the end she was just a couple of embers and a wisp of a breath. Acquaintances and family just saw us as friends, or companions, and if they suspected otherwise no one said anything. We never 'came out' to the gas board. It didn't seem appropriate.

What now? That's what I wanted to know.

One day I wandered into an area of the city that was filled with fatherly banks, The Mercenaries Wives Investment Bank, The Golden Bank of Cairo. I admired a row of devilish gargoyles that leered down from its cornices. Then I passed a large Victorian building and smelt wet towel and steam. Through a glass door I could see a demure elderly woman sitting behind a sign that said 'Tuesday is Ladies Day in the Turkish Baths.'

At least it would be snug, I thought, and anonymous.

Ladies Day was very cheap, much cheaper than Thursday apparently, which was mixed. For a moment I imagined mixed days. Huge bellies of hairy men, sweat running down their enormous foreheads.

The demure woman was staring at me. I paid and she gave me a ticket, a towel and a hanger.

I walked slowly down a flight of steps. I could smell sodden towel and skin. I felt a bit unsure. It was all a bit quick. I walked into a carpeted room, warmish, with botanical plastic plants and a row of cubicles. They had green velvet curtains. A wiry woman in a bathing costume with long breasts was watching television. She widened her eyes and pointed at a sign that said 'Changing.' The air was chewy. I drifted on into a cubicle. There was a bed, a white pillow and a mirror set in the dark wood. I looked at myself. I was the colour of ash, and my eyes were dull and bloodshot. My clothes peeled off in unwashed slabs.

My blue-white body was sharp and angular. It was shrivelled in some places. I held the small, hired white towel against my gas board breasts, and walked out and towards the chambers. I could hear a kind of rumbling, as if beneath us there was a great boiler burping steam into the tiled rooms.

I found myself in the first chamber. I could hardly see anything. I stared through the vapourish mist, and managed to make out the mountainous shapes of two vastly-naked women, one slouched on the bench reading a novel, and the other stood in the corner, feet apart, beating herself with birch twigs. I sat down wrapped in my shrimp of a towel.

I nodded, then stared at the skin on my arm. It was oozing something green and yellow.

'What's that?' I squeaked.

The reader didn't even look up from her book.

'Sorrow,' she said.

Calidarium.

It took me nearly ten minutes to get out of the front door. All the locks were iced up. It's very difficult pouring boiling water into a keyhole. In the end I used the iron. When I stepped outside my neighbour who was cutting her hedge with a pair of kitchen scissors gave me a pitying look.

I walked carefully through puddles of cracked ice. The bus was filled with wet umbrellas and moist gassy vapours.

When I got to the baths the large naked reader was holding a copy of 'Moby Dick'. She nodded at me, held out her hand and said 'I'm Francie, that's Irene,' pointing at the twig woman who was rubbing something greasy into her navel with a circular movement.

An Indian woman swathed in black plastic lay silently on a deck chair. Three sweet-faced girls sat in a close and naked circle discussing stars. I bravely entered the Calidarium; even hotter than the first room. A sheet of dry heat enclosed me. Every orifice quivered with shock.

I sat down on the burning wooden bench and let my heart melt. My skin began to drip and Francie came in, padding over the straw mats with her brown feet.

I thought she was going to speak, but she sat down and stared ahead as if she was in some kind of trance.

I drifted off again, thinking about Mel. She was standing in blue shorts halfway up some steps, telling me to hurry up, or riding on the top deck of an open bus with her hair standing up, dressed in white against a green carpet of grass, stubbing out a French cigarette with her flat shoe.

I was there in every picture. I'm not there now, wherever she is. Francie touched me lightly on the shoulder.

'Long enough,' she said, and when I got up I was dizzy and could hardly walk straight. Mel's death swam about in front of my eyes.

Irene looked up as I staggered back to the cooler chamber.

'You alright?'

'I just miss my friend,' I mumbled deliriously. A whoosh of steam obscured her response.

After that I slept in the steam and dreamt that I was in bed with Mel. She said she wanted cigarettes. I reached over and touched her arm.

'Your hands are very warm,' she said, and moved. But it wasn't me that was warm, it was her that was turning cold.

When I opened my eyes Francie was lying reading a newspaper, and Irene was slumped on a marble slab being scrubbed and pummelled by a heavy handed woman in a blue overall.

Irene spoke with her languorous eyes closed.

'It's amazing what the body stores up,' she muttered, then threw over a tube of cream. 'Rub that in,' she said, turning her head away.

The cream was cool. I began to cry.

Laconium.

I passed Irene in the street today. She looked completely different. She was wearing a wig and a smart black gown, and clipping along by the Crown Court. She must be a barrister, or even a judge. She looked very intimidating. I was amazed that I had had the privilege of seeing her with nothing on. I lifted my hand warily to wave, but she didn't see me.

I looked at myself. I nearly looked like a tramp, but I think I was saved by my shoes which were still polished.

Lately I have been aware that I have another self, beneath my clothes, which breathes and thinks quite independently to the ordinary me, the woman who creeps down the street.

When I got to the baths Francie was there as usual, but the day was slightly spoilt by a party of what looked like theology students, all gazing gloomily into the steam, with small fragile breasts and young white teeth.

That was why I followed Francie into the Laconium.

It was the hottest chamber. A small yellow tiled room in the heart of the baths. It was so hot that I was afraid that I might start to cook.

Francie closed her eyes. I did too. I let the sorrow come out of me and drip down into the veins and arteries of the city. I could hear it sobbing in the sewers. And for a moment there was nothing but heat, and the molten grief of warm women. I imagined it steaming up through the gutters, smelling of sweat and tears and dirt and overpowering the city. Like tear gas. Then I had a sensation of being carried down a river. I felt weepy. All I ever wanted was warmth.

I let my shoulders slump, and my mouth slip open.

My heart galloped so loud I thought I might have a heart attack, and I didn't care.

When I opened my eyes Francie was smiling at me.

Her face was kind. She had thick, suburban eyebrows and plump shoulders. Her eyes were the colour of pilot lights.

She stood up.

'I've got work to do,' she said, picking up her towel. 'See you.'

'Work?' I said. The word burning up like a struck match.

'I fix boilers,' said Francie. 'French ones.'

Eamon McDonnell

Short-listed in the 1996/97 Fish Short Story Prize

was born of mixed race, one parent Catholic the other Protestant. His earliest memories are of the sound of the Lambeg drum, apparently in July, and of a nice policeman. He grew to dislike the music of the former and found he was not to refer to the latter.

As a teenager, in Belfast, he considered there was more to life than side-stepping buildings falling into the street so skipped to Dublin, though not for long. He went to London to check out the pavements for gold only to learn that a bunch of Irish navvies had asset-stripped them in the last century. He remains in London to this day having recently given up the nine-to-five boredom to attempt writing full-time.

Tricky Journey

Eamon McDonnell

It was a complete bloody waste. That was the match post-mortem in the dressing room. All the way across the city to be beaten by a mindless penalty to a bunch of fat-arsed Protestants. Brian, team captain, had a way with words. But he was right about the penalty. Terry had out-jumped our keeper and caught the damn ball.

'Why did you do it, Terry?'

'I was bored.'

It's a mistake not to appreciate how a man can love football. Terry did and Brian knocked him out cold with his great crunch of a fist. The rest of us sat there, not a flinch between us.

Later I stood at the bus stop with Brian, not a word had passed between us since I'd picked Terry up off the floor.

'You saving words up for a novel or something, Sean?'

'No,' I replied.

'I had to hit him, mate or not.'

'I'd call him a not from now on.'

'It's about discipline. There comes a time when you have to use force to make your point, like. Are you with me?'

'Oh yeah. Get on the bus here.'

'No. I'm walking.'

'It's five miles in the sheeting rain. And it's a tricky journey. If you know what I mean.'

'So?'

And with that Brian dandered off in his bow-legged fashion, his black steel toe-capped boots tapping on the grey paving stones as he walked.

Isn't this just like life? One minute you're with twelve mates shouting and laughing the next you're sitting on your own on a bus full of strange Protestants.

It is the gift of God that we Ulster folk can tell another's religion by scanning their eyebrows. It's more difficult with women though, as they pluck theirs, like ginger-haired Lucy, the lust of my life. It was her fault I couldn't run the length of myself today.

God don't get a horn on in front of that old lady she could jam those knitting needles up your scrotum before you could apologise. The sooner I get out of Indian country the better. And right on cue the bus broke to a halt sending the old lady up the aisle of the bus and her skirt up to the nape of her neck. Thank God she was fully clothed underneath.

'This bus is being commandeered by the Irish Republican Army,' said a voice no more than twelve.

'You little shite,' said a dapper old man as he hit the child over the head with an umbrella.

There was a brief cheer, then silence, when a balaclava head stepped on to the bus, rifle in arms.

'We're setting this bus alight.'

'Alight here then,' someone shouted.

Balaclava head walked down the bus slowly turning his head like a tank turret.

He stopped at me. It would be okay, all he had to do was look at my eyebrows.

Smack! His rifle butt spun off my forehead and I was on the floor.

'Alight head now, funny man,' Balaclava said.

Then he kicked me deep into my bollocks. The pain instantly left my head, shot to my groin, then my stomach heaved up into my throat. The old lady had got to her feet.

'Leave the wee lad alone, you Fenian bollocks.'

I wanted to tell her not to provoke Balaclava but the only words that came out in my delirium were:

'Needles... his scrotum.'

And by that time Balaclava had gone and the smell of petrol was everywhere. Some kind passengers had carried me over to a cafe and sat me in the window where I could watch the bus go up. I told them they were very kind. Beside me plonked a man in dungarees and moustache; his corpulence pressing my right arm useless against my side. He leaned into me peering through his bottle-top glasses, firing lager fumes into the back of my throat.

'I'm Dixon. Do you see that? Of course you do. But do you see it?'

'Yes,' I said. If in doubt, be positive.

'I doubt if you do. Will I tell you why?'

Could I stop you?

'That is a bus on fire. Right? Right. But it's more than that. That is an act of war and as an act of war all young men should be enlisted into the forces of right and justice. Are you a member?'

'No. Not really.'

'What d'ya mean? Not really. Do you wanna join?'

It's got to be a trick question. Is he checking out my eyebrows? Perhaps they'd welcome me as a member. The first full-time Catholic member of the Ulster Volunteer Force: I could do administrative work for them once I passed my 'A' levels.

'Do you want to join?'

He said this with the precision stupid people use when trying to get deaf people to hear what they are saying.

'What are you saying to that wee lad? He's had a traumatic experience.'

'Aye, he has.' A red face.

95

'Some git rifled him.' A mother pogoing a babe in arms.

'Went through his trousers like?' A puzzled voice from under a scarf.

'You'd like to, I know.' Whoever that was.

'Please ladies. No thing rude in my cafe,' said the little Italian man.

'If it wasn't for your Pope there wouldn't be any of this trouble.'

'He is not my Pope. I tell you again and again. I am Protestant.'

'An Italian Protestant. Did you ever hear the like of that?' Dixon nudged me.

'He doesn't know the first thing about black pudding.' Obviously not a member.

The cafe door opened and in walked two policemen. Dixon threw his just lit cigarette into the ashtray. 'Must be going,' and made a beeline to the Gents.

The police walked over to me as I made a mental note to pluck my eyebrows and stop all this fretting. All they wanted to do was give me a lift home which I declined because of the obvious peculiarity of my address; but accepted one to the City Hall which was near enough to Lucy: perpetual lust of my life. Once she took me in her arms, all would be well. Only she could tell me if my cock was broken for life.

I stumbled to my feet putting one arm around the police constable and hobbled to the door.

'No bag or anything?' asked the Police sergeant.

'Yeah. My football gear...' I looked across at the burning bus and remembered where I had left it. 'They've burnt it. The bastards.' Which was greeted with spontaneous applause by the customers in the cafe. I hobbled out the door with:

'He's a hero that wee lad.' Singing in my ears.

The journey down to City Hall was quick. It was the only way to travel if you were out and about and in and around the RUC. They were talkative in an RUC kind of way. What's your name? where do you live? what were you doing on the bus? why did you limp into the cafe? the people that carried you there were they known to you? do you usually accept help from total strangers? do you not think that unwise given the particular security situation in Our Province at present? what did you say your father did? what is his name...?

'City Hall. This do you?'

You could have dropped me off sooner. I calculated that I had lied every thirty feet travelling at a constant speed of forty-five miles per hour for eleven and one half minutes. Fast tracking to Hell.

As the constable helped me out of the Land-Rover I stumbled and fell.

'Look at that black Protestant bastard beating the crap out of the wee fellah. Chuck that brick.'

In the distance I could see the brick getting bigger and bigger until it bounced off the grey roof of the Land-Rover.

'Get back in for God's sake.'

'No officer. Save yourself. I'll be okay.'

The constable hesitated for about three bricks, jumped back in the Land-Rover and was away. Now I was surrounded by my own kind. I could see the gold twinkle of the Connolly badges on their lapels. They leant over me, expectantly. I didn't have to say anything. They told my tale.

'What happened to ye?'

'Can't you see the lump on his head?'

'Lotta blood on his shirt.'

'He can barely walk they kicked him in the back of that Land-Rover so much.'

'Evil bastards.'

'They were probably going to shoot him...'

'Until we stopped it.'

'What did you do to make them pick you up in the first place?'

'Since when do you have to do something before those bastards pick you up?'

I could see a familiar face coming at me through the crowd.

'Do you never say bugger all, Sean?'

'I never get the bloody chance, Brian. Take me to Kelly's Cellars and help me shovel pints.'

'Sure. Where's your kit?'

'Left it on a bus.'

'Careless twat.'

'At least I didn't concede a penalty.'

'That doesn't matter a shite. It was only a friendly.'

I wasn't following any of this. The sooner I got ensconced at Kelly's the better. Sit down, let my balls stop aching then go to my Lucy. God how I wanted her. And God did it hurt when I thought of her like that.

After much limping and whining on my part we got into the bar. Nobody in. Gerry was behind the bar his arms spread across the counter.

'Gerry, two pints of Black Label,' I said.

'If I were you lads I'd beat a retreat home. The peasants are in revolt. The Bs shot some bloke or something. Anyway, it's all up the yard. I'm just waiting for the boss to give me the word to get out. Two pints you say?'

'Aye.'

Gerry was known to exaggerate. He once had everyone believing that the British Legion had a military wing which had taken over the province and had people stationed on every street in Ulster. It turned out to be British Legion flag day. But it was surprising the amount of people that wanted to believe him. Anyway, there was Brian and me sitting in the snug corner when the window flew in chased by a blast of air and a bang. We looked over to where Gerry had been standing then found ourselves in a crumpled heap on the floor.

Neither of us had been in a bomb explosion before, not even on the periphery like this. We were neither stunned nor shocked, more a kind of clueless. The first thing we tried to do was stand up. A mistake. Our legs were quivering like jelly; a jelly that has set on an outside ledge. Gerry looked over us.

'Don't get up boys until you can feel all your bits working. Any strangeness?'

'Aye,' I said. 'I've got a ringing in my ears.'

'That's the burglar alarms.'

'Fuck all use going off now. Why don't they go off when they see the thing planted?'

Brian was right. Once the damage is done, off go the alarms; like who's not going to notice a six storey building falling to the ground.

'Get up Brian.'

He lay motionless on the legless top of a table, plaster dust covering him like caster sugar over a chocolate log.

'I'm going to stay here. I'm going to contemplate seriousness. How drink can kill you, inadvertently. And maybe even is there any purpose in football for the eighteen year old. What d'you think?'

'I think you've had a bang on the head. Gerry, get him a Babycham.'

'Not content with seeing him have his arse blown across an uncrowded pub they then set about to poison the poor bastard. Leave me be. Go and give your leggy Lucy one. Think of all the sympathy you'll get. The limp; the disfigured balls; the cut hands...'

I hadn't noticed the blood trickling out from under my shirt cuff into my curled fingers.

'And his head is cut as well.'

'Indeed it always has been Gerry, but Lucy minds not. Isn't that right Sean?'

I smiled. Listened to the sirens. The bells. The hum of speeding vehicles and decided Lucy was my salvation. I would offer my pain and agony to her as a sacrifice, in the hope that she would take her knickers down for me.

It was a bitch that she lived in the Divis Tower. Especially on a night like this. With my brain in my pants I strode up the Lower Falls. People everywhere. Staring at me. A Neanderthal speaks as he walks towards me. No mean feat in itself.

'Hey you. What the fuck are you doing around here?'

The first thing you must realise, when engaging a Neanderthal, is that you are not being asked a question. Secondly, and somewhat obliquely, you are not being confronted by a member of the Northern Ireland Tourist Board. So what is it about?

It is about the fact that unless you think quickly you are about to get an almighty kicking. Given my precarious state of health the Clitheroe Kid could have kicked seven bells out of me so one must recourse to the devious. Observe. When approached by a Neanderthal, in a busy Belfast street, smile widely and wave, looking beyond said Neanderthal towards a passer-by. Shout the phrase: 'Bout you Jimmy.'

Said passer-by will stop, squint, then wave back. For strangely, although few people are actually called Jimmy, in Ulster, almost all of the male population respond to the name as though it were their own.

During this exchange the Neanderthal will stop and turn around looking at the 'Jimmy' of your choosing.

It is at this point that you duck down the first side street you can find hopefully to the Neanderthal strains of, 'Hey Jimmy. How come you know yer man?'

Head down hands in pockets listening to bangs and thumps and raps invisibly painting themselves across the black sky. Kids under the block dancing on a scorched car beating the shell of it with broom handles longer than themselves. Up the stairwell wet with urine. Upward, ever upward towards Lucy's door. Let her be in God. Will God permit her to be at home to enact scenes of perversity? Me, lost in the thought of her long red hair. Christ! What's that I've fallen over?

'Look where you're going you silly wee bastard.'

A man in black. Holding a rifle. This is not my day. Say nothing. Say: 'Sorry.'

Go like hell, but do it casually. Lucy's door. Make for Lucy's door. Knock it firmly, gently. What's keeping her? The lights are out. But then all the lights are out.

Then the door opens.

Slowly.

'What are you doing here? There's snipers all over the block.'

'I know. I fell over one. Let me in. I'm aching for you. Literally.'

'No. Go home it's too dangerous.' Her soft voice turning my mouth to sandpaper.

'My marriage tackle has been blunted by Republicanism.'

'Oh yeah.'

'Don't be so flippant Lucy McMahon. I've come through Hades to be here.'

'You poor thing.'

Gently Lucy lowered my zip and with her strange power recovered my manhood. I genuflected at her naked white thighs and buried my face up into her short loose skirt and lifted her into the air, kicking open the door.

'No don't,' she whispered gruffly.

I knew she didn't mean it. I walked down the short corridor, her thighs wriggling around my head. A few more seconds and we'd be on the sofa; the one we'd broken the springs of.

'For Christ sake stop.'

I'd already stopped. I could swear I heard bottles clinking. And the smell of petrol. I lowered Lucy off my face. Milk bottles with rags in them. Three men frozen, staring at me. One of the men I recognised.

'Hello, Mr. McMahon.'

'I'll give you hello, you dirty wee scoundrel.'

'Sean! For shit's sake run!'

Lucy's advice shook me from paralysis. God how I love her.

And did I run? Out the door so fast, unable to turn, into the wall, lurching over, looking down below. Below at the army looking up.

'There he is, sir.'

Oh no. Run, run, run. Get down the stairs. Two at a time. Four at a time. Leap. My ears pounding with blood, my groin wanting to wet itself. The burnt-out car. Dive over the boot through the windowless back. Crouched. Gasping for air I try to stop breathing. Don't be heard. A noise. Footsteps. A bang on the side of the car. I jump.

I race through an interrogation. No I'm not a sniper. Why did I run? Yes why did I run? No I don't live anywhere near here. My parents. My father!

A forehead and a small pair of eyes peep over the car door at me.

'We're playing here. Burn your own car out.' Says a six year old.

'The Brits are after me,' I almost beg.

'We'll get rid of them. Finbar, Rory get some bricks. Soldiers are going to chase us.'

I hear two tiny cheers.

I waited. Listened. Heard the bricks hit against something. Heard the chorus of children laughing. Heard heavy boots running into the distance. Started to breathe again, wrenching the air into my face.

'Get home. Get home,' I chanted like a mantra.

Every street black. Every doorway threatening to open on me. The slightest cat stops my stride. I hear footsteps. In the distance. Getting closer. So loud the person should be standing beside me now. It's not footsteps. It's a hundred footsteps. A gang of youths running round the corner. I look for a door with the light on. There must be one. There is. I run over to it. Pray they haven't spotted me. I lean against the door. Shaking, I light a cigarette. They begin to run past. I smile. They shout.

'Come on we've caught one of the bastards.' One of them

stops in front of me. I recognise him. It is Neanderthal.

'Don't I know you?'

'Yes. How are things?'

'Great. We've caught one. Come on and we'll give him a hiding.'

'Can't. My mother's inside, sick. Only came out for a fag.'

'Right. Hope she gets better. See ya.'

The stampede moves down the street. The door behind me opens. I turn and face a man in pyjama bottoms, vest and braces: a cigarette jammed into the right hand side of his mouth. He talks through his teeth.

'What are you doing?'

'Having a fag.'

'Well fuck off and have it somewhere else.'

This social disorder is destroying the notion of Irish hospitality. Who cares, almost safe. Another mile ought to do it. A hum inside my head. It's getting louder. It's pulling alongside me. Will I look?

'Hey boy. Do you want a lift?'

It's a milk float. Driven by a what? Fourteen year old? Take the lift.

'I'm heading for Fruithill.'

'Dead on. That's where this buggy is headed.'

I jump up. Lie stretched out across the back. Who cares if I'm arrested. I'm too tired. I need a nice warm padded cell.

'Where's the milk bottles then?'

'Are you taking the piss?'

End of conversation until we arrive at Fruithill.

Outside my house a double-decker bus is parked. We're not on a bus route. My driver calls over to his mates sitting on the bus.

'Transport home lads.'

I walk up to my front door and gently turn the key and tip-toe in. I can hear muffled voices coming from the sitting room. I open the sitting room door and in the light of a candle are kneeling

Mum, Dad, my four brothers and sisters and granny. They are saying the rosary.

Mum: 'Bring Sean home safe to us.'

Chorus: 'God bring us peace.'

Sis: 'Don't let them burn down my school with my special painting in it.'

Chorus: 'God bring us peace.'

I gently close the door and go into the dark of the front room.

I stand, arms folded, staring out the window. I watch the bus burn.

Getting anywhere is going to be tricky from now on.

Geraldine Mills

Runner-up in the 1996/97 Fish Short Story Prize

I am the sole member of the Galway Branch of St. Colmcilles Writers'
Workshop, Tallaght, Dublin, where I lived for twenty years before
coming *Into the West*. My writing takes me beyond the confines of my
kitchen walls to far-flung places and prize winning ceremonies. You could
call me a 'near miss' (or Ms.) having enough 'Highly Commended'
Awards to paper my tree house. Though my talent has been acclaimed as
far afield as Ballyhaunis, Cootehill, Listowel, Wexford and Scotland, the
big win is only a hen's kick away. I like to write about obsessions,
betrayal and earthworms.

World Of Trees

Geraldine Mills

To Esme it seems that the woman has caught her in her gaze. She is staring out of the television so directly at her that Esme cannot look away. With her dark eyes and the way her hair curls in grey across her forehead she reminds her of Mrs McManus who used to live in the house that backed onto theirs when she was a little girl. Esme remembers her eyes because they were the colour of earth. The same coloured eyes are looking at her again. This earth-eyed woman is saying something in a language that Esme does not understand. There is a doctor checking her heart, her pulse, her tongue, and over her voice the interpreter is telling the world that it is her first time in four years that she has been among people. There is nothing in her face to show this. In fact she looks so ordinary you would think she was about to take out a bowl and make bread or reach down for her Brasso to polish her front door. The male voice brakes her Slavic dialect. Esme is stopped in her tracks and sits on the edge of the couch, her little daughter's sock still in her hand. In a strange country voice he is telling her that she was four years in the forest and now she has come back.

Esme leaves the room and goes out by the patio doors to the garden. There is a thumbnail of moon as clean as a nun's. The weeping willow trails down into the corner. Esme sits on the garden chair. The one with the arm tied together with an old nylon stocking and looks back at the house. There are three lights on. Beatrice's room, their own bedroom, the living room. From here she can still see the television flickering.

When Beatrice came, Paul went back on the cigarettes. He had been doing really well and had been off them for two years. Nearly. Now all his defences were down and she knew it was only a matter of time. She can see his shadow walk back and forth behind the blind in their room. He is biding his time, wondering what to do. Beatrice is lying on her bed, knees bent, arrowed towards the ceiling, blowing clouds of smoke onto her mirror while she contemplates her next move. Beatrice always has a next move.

Beatrice has come back from London with no job and no partner. There was nothing new in that, for jobs and lovers were discarded like tights that were threatening to ladder. She suffered the three-year itch rather than the statutory seven. Ordinarily Esme would have been more cautious having her sister arrive at her door like that but she presented herself just as there was a crisis in the childminding arrangements. The most recent one had rung the day before to say she was going walkabout in Australia and Esme was in a sweat as to who would look after Richard and Melanie. She couldn't take any time off work with the deadline for the new project so close and the local crèche was overflowing. Beatrice was born with her life insurance policy clenched in her tiny fist and she moved into Richard's yellow room with the dinosaur curtains. Crisis over, the house settled with relief.

Beatrice would not eat beef. No one was eating it in London now and she didn't care even if their butcher personally autographed every rump steak. She wasn't going to let her brains go so spongy that she would be falling around the place as if she'd had a margarita too many. If her legs were going from under her she wanted it to have been a pleasurable experience and not through the consumption of burning bovine flesh. Esme had to rearrange her weekly shopping list, fobbing off the children with turkey burgers instead. Beatrice wondered if a television in her room would be too much trouble so Paul moved the portable from their room into the little yellow one and set it up on the pine shelf beside the wardrobe.

Esme does not like the lights shining down on her. She takes the chair with its arm in a sling and carries it in under the willow tree. The moon shines through the branches. She likes the feel of the trees, tentacles hanging down around her. No one will ever find her here. It is summer and the weather is good. She can still see out but anyone coming into the garden would think they had it to themselves. Has she the wherewithal she wonders to sleep a sound sleep here under the tree? A makeshift home camouflaged by branches and moss. Keeping little or nothing out. The shadow of the woman from the television crosses the moon, comes in beside her, covers her hands with knowing. Helps her.

Beatrice loved her cigarettes. She placed her Gauloises on the coffee table with the silver lighter settled neatly on top while Esme stacked the dishwasher. Paul sat watching her while she slipped the long cigarette out of its pack, placed it between her lips, let the flame engulf the tip while she drew in the air of ignition. He sat there pretending he was not being drawn in, pretending with each drag that he wasn't being drawn in. He declined her first few offers. Put his hands up in cruciform defence as if he were warding off a vampire. He was showing great discipline. Letting on it didn't matter. And then one evening Esme came in and saw twin spirals of smoke rise towards the ceiling and mingle. In fact Esme isn't quite sure which came first. The cigarette or the fall.

The woman's shadow settles in around Esme. She hears Paul come out onto the patio and call her name. Once. Twice. She does not answer. Let him think she has gone. She does not want to talk to him. She doesn't want to hear his reasoning. Telling her it is all in her imagination. She is more interested in the television woman. How did she deal with knowing of the fierce weather that was to come or the wild dogs that scavenged at night? How did she sleep knowing that soldiers had ripped apart her family, that her father too old to defend himself, had been blasted to pieces, her daughter pregnant and little Rula ripe for the picking? How would you sleep at night knowing that they might come this far into the forest to look for you? Hearing in the far-off town the explosion of shells. The war sounds. Bridges burning so that there was no turning back.

Around Beatrice, Paul and herself were like two chemical reagents that were bubbling away in a scientist's round bottomed flask on a lab bench somewhere. Beatrice, like the good old catalyst that she was, speeded up the reaction and remained virtually unchanged while all around her feelings bubbled and foamed and the final product was unrecognisable from the first. Beatrice was still intact to go on to the next experiment.

Paul carried himself differently. He was more vocal, more lively. This wasn't the way he would be normally after three days on the road. BB, or Before Beatrice he would come in and dump his frayed temper and baggage on the floor, flop into the chair and Esme would wait until he slowly became acclimatised to the domesticity around him.

Now he came in, hung his coat in the cloakroom and poured them all a drink. Then Beatrice offered a cigarette and his hand came across to shelter hers, slipped one from the packet as she flashed open her lighter and they both drew a long satisfied sigh. To Esme she couldn't be more sure than if she were watching them naked in their bed.

Inside the cover of the willow tree, Esme sees the woman of Sarajevo, her teeth green from the leaves she has been chewing, some of them broken from the hard shell of nuts, the purple tint of berries on her hands. In the cold of winter did she try to burrow into the ground, roll up her body like a squirrel and wait till the earth turned and threw up the new light of Spring? How did she keep a handle on her time, pressing words out of her mind unused, left without air, unless she unleashed them onto the birds or beetles that scurried into corners? All her words that she would have fallen over as a little girl. Stumbling over niceties of language like please and thank you. Superfluous now, while her head filled with words like pain and loss and fear. She could have sung songs to keep the wolves of panic at bay. Dragging out old lullabies that never got past the first refrain before they got shadowed by that first morning. A new calendar started for her then, from the moment she heard the shots when she was in the outhouse. The shots of the Serb soldiers coming to wipe out her family. She ran the length of the yard through the gap in the fence that opened into a track overgrown with brambles into the forest. She kept running till she found a place deep within the trees. A world of trees that had never been felled by foresters since man first came, swallowing the dead for centuries. Wagons from 1812, bits of leather straps and buttons scattered all around, disintegrating into moss. There she spent the day putting stones together building a shelter. A home that was to last her four years until a hunter passing through the woods came upon her and told her that the war was over. She did not trust his word for there was nothing but night and day that she was sure of now. It was only when he returned a second time some months later with the same news that she found somewhere within herself to believe him. Now the world knew of her survival.

Esme tells her that life will never be the same again. The light from her will shine at a different frequency after this. Different from the morning in the outhouse when, having first fed her father, wiping the saliva from his mouth, touching Marya's growing stomach and feeling the baby stir, telling Rula to keep the fire going... and when the hunter came four years later, 1,461 days or over five million seconds, how many had she counted? How many names had she thrown into the night to her unborn grandchild?

When Paul was away his car rested in the carport. He didn't like Esme to drive it. He was adamant that it was too big for her. Yet she watched him adjusting the seat for Beatrice so that she could reach the pedals, and getting her on his insurance so that she could drive it. When she tackled him he laughed and told her she was jealous. That there was no point in having a car idle in the drive when Beatrice could do the shopping and pick up the kids from their fun group on rainy days. It would just make her own life easier. She wouldn't have to go out to the shops when she had only come in from work. He said her imagination would be the end of her.

Esme feels the evening chill settle around her. The woman from Sarajevo is lying on the ground. The cold will swell up from the earth and surge through her bones. Esme takes off her cardigan and lays it on her. She covers her ears so that they won't hear the gunfire.

She has watched him evening after evening, his eyes bright, sitting across the dinner table and talking to her sister in a way that they once did together. Especially in those years before the children came along, when her cheeks were warm with wine and they didn't notice night falling slow. The look on his face now is a look she remembers from a long time ago when it was solely for her. A look that had got buried somewhere along the line.

Standing at her window she studied them as they came back along the path from an evening walk, he bending his frame to catch her words. Esme watched him, caught between light and dark, while he bent down and picked a sprig of lavender and held it under her nose. It was as if he had just woken up to a whole new world. One that she mustn't be able to offer. It was the way they came in laughing, the coolness of the evening wrapped around them. Paul rubbing his hands together to get the circulation going.

'Any chance of a cup of coffee Es? It's getting chilly out there.'

'The children are waiting for you to read them a story. You promised.'

'Couldn't you do it tonight?'

'No I couldn't.'

'Right then, be back in a min. Have the coffee ready, maybe a drop of brandy in it.'

Beatrice went over and put the kettle on. Esme stopped her as she took down the cups.

'The agency rang me today, it looks like they have a babyminder that would be suitable, so you should start looking for a real job.'

'But I thought you liked having me here. Richard and Melanie love their auntie. Do you really want to put them through that again when they are so settled?'

'I am sure you would be much happier if you had your own place. Maybe London is missing you.'

'What are you trying to say to me Es?'

'Don't call me Es.'

'Right sister dear. Out with it.'

'Are you sleeping with Paul?'

'What on earth makes you ask that?'

'I don't need regression therapy to remember your past.'

'Don't you think that's a bit below the belt?'

'Well are you?'

'I think your husband is the best one to answer that.'

Esme climbs the stairs. She hears Paul finishing the story for their children. The Billy Goats Gruff are getting the better of the troll and when they kick him up in the air, he burns up as he falls back through the atmosphere. Richard added that bit of reality to the fairytale. He couldn't understand how it could be otherwise since astronauts had to be very careful when they did it. She stands at their door. Richard has his thumb in his mouth, Melanie is already asleep. They're getting older but they're still their babies. She bends and picks up Melanie's sock that's on the floor by the door. She sees the marks on the door that measure their spurts of growth. There's Richard's and below him Melanie's. Two new marks have been etched into the stripped pine, way above their children's. Paul's at five foot eleven and below that by a good three inches, Beatrice's. They had carved themselves forever into her house.

She is standing in the bathroom screaming at Paul. He tells her she is imagining things. She's his sister-in-law for God's sake. She confronts him with the carving on the children's door frame. He laughs. It was only a bit of fun. But his name is lying on top of hers. The way he wants it to be. She asks him has he slept with her. He says no. She wants to believe him but she knows by the way he holds his head and he rubs his index finger along his top lip that it is not the full truth. She tells him that she has found a new childminder. That they don't need Beatrice's services any more. She has told her to go. She sees the look of hate sear into his face and disappear. He cannot argue this one. He has always left the childminding arrangements to her. If he says anything he will give it all away. She leaves and goes downstairs. She sees the light on in Beatrice's room. As she goes through the living room she is stopped by the earth-eyed woman.

From her covert she watches the woman from Sarajevo who came back after four years, with the spirit to pick up the pieces, search the faces of village people that might have the same line of jaw, the same forehead, or colour eyes, so that she could tell if they were from her own lineage. Esme had nothing like that spirit. Until now.

From here she can see the light go out in their bedroom. Paul walking along the corridor. Knocking on Beatrice's door. Going into the room with its yellow walls and dinosaurs and lying the full length of the bed with her.

Pat Boran

Runner-up in the 1996/97 Fish Short Story Prize

Born in Portlaoise in 1963. He has published three full-length collections of poems, *The Unwound Clock* (1990), *Familiar Things* (1993), and *The Shape of Water* (1996). He has also published a collection of short stories, *Strange Bedfellows (1991)*.

Florence - The Rough Guide

Pat Boran

Sounded like a great idea. At the time. Me and Florence - sorry, me and Flo; sorry, Flo and I - on a dirty weekend in (wait for it) Florence. Where else? Cost me a packet, okay, but what man could resist it? A real, passionate woman of flesh *and* the mother of the Italian Renaissance - at the same time. As I say, sounded like a great idea. At the time.

HISTORY

I first met Florence, or Flo as she prefers to be called, in London. Like all momentous encounters, it happened quite casually. She was standing waiting for a bus near Piccadilly, and so was I. She looked kind of interesting, fishnet stockings, the lot. I said something like, 'Excuse me, but do you have a light?' And that was it. That was all it took. From there we adjourned to a small Italian place for a meal, and eventually back to her place. The affair lasted the whole weekend I was over to see Tottenham Hotspur.

When those few fantastic days were over I came back to Dublin, back to my job in Dublin Bus, while Flo stayed on in her squeaky-clean apartment in Hampstead, staring into her computer screen, walking barefoot across the polished floors, remote-controlling her slim-line hi-fi, being reflected occasionally in her tropical fish tank, reading someone called Naomi Wolf in her water bed (I swear to God!) or soaking in the bath under a huge print of what she informed me was Botticelli's *Primavera*. Flo is very much an outdoor type, as I would discover later. Even her apartment smelt of woods and meadows.

As is probably obvious by now, I couldn't get her out of my mind. That's when I had my great idea. That's when I phoned her and asked her if she'd come away with me.

'Love to, Fran,' she said to my amazement. Two weeks later we were on our way.

ARRIVAL AND GETTING AROUND

We decided to skip Rome and fly direct to Pisa. An uncle of mine, I told Flo, had a friend who got mugged in Rome once. Anyway, from London it's possible to fly just about anywhere direct, one of the few good things about the place. Flo had been kind of keen on seeing the Eternal City, I think, but in the end she saw the sense of my argument.

'Anyway,' I added, 'if it's really eternal, it'll still be there if we come back some other time.'

Arriving in Florence itself isn't too bad - though a couple of extra toilets in the station wouldn't go amiss.

'What was wrong with the one on the train?' Flo said as I paced up and down in the station.

'I told you,' I said.

What was I supposed to do if a conductor came along and started babbling at me in Italian or demanding the tickets that Flo insisted on holding onto for safe-keeping? A man could find himself locked up in some dungeon for the rest of his life with only homosexuals and drug smugglers for company. I'd seen the films. I'd heard the stories.

So we took a taxi to our accommodation though, in less strained circumstances, I'd have preferred to take a bus, just to see what they were like over there. As it was, the taxi cost us a small fortune: either all the streets are alike, or we passed the same one about twenty times before the driver decided to let us out. He was probably getting dizzy going around in circles! I was hoping I hadn't done my bladder permanent damage.

FINDING A PLACE TO STAY

The hotel would have been fine - nice and central, just across the river, lots of young people of all nationalities around, a lot of them female, I must admit, and very attractive - except that it wasn't a hotel.

'Ostello!' said Flo. 'Hostel.' Then she did her pronunciation thing. 'I don't hear an 's' in hotel, do you?'

'I didn't hear an 's' in Ostello,' I said. 'What am I supposed to be, multilingual?'

Flo looked at me darkly while the receptionist balanced a single plucked eyebrow in the air for what must have been minutes.

I thought I'd try a joke to break the deadlock. I really couldn't see the point in getting worked up about it.

'And if I could read cuneiform as well,' I said, ' would that make me cunnilingual?'

'Do you want the rooms, or not?' said the receptionist in perfect English. It was late, we were hungry, we had no choice. I spent my first night in Florence with seven German men and two snoring Danes. Flo slept with nine Miss Americas. She hardly spoke to me the following day. We checked out of the hostel - *Arrivederci Yeah, yeah, ciao* - booked into a hotel across the way using Flo's Visa card as the sole form of communication, and sat silently in our room, wondering where the excitement had gone.

Later Flo calmed down and we ate pizza like there was no tomorrow. The pizza was thin and crackly. Mean on the extras. The restaurant was on the side of the river where the hotel was, the side the locals call the Oltrarno, or the other side of the Arno, which is the river. I couldn't figure that out. If one side was called the other side, what was the other side called? I wanted to ask the waiter. If he wouldn't give us a good thick pizza, we might as well get some information from him. Flo, who had taken to the local vino like a fish to water, said to just forget it.

THE CITY

The thing to see in Florence is art. It's just about everywhere. Art and churches. Not, of course, that you can separate one from the other. The Renaissance - which really means rebirth - actually may have all been about painting and fruit and horses and stuff, and guys lying on their backs for days on end getting the twiddly bits right, but who do you think financed most of it, or a hell of a lot of it at least? That's right. The church. And - and this is where things began to get really difficult to explain to Flo - not just any church. It wasn't as if there were a whole lot of churches competing to give work to the painters and sculptors and models who were hanging around on the bread line. It wasn't as if there was a choice of churches willing to shell out for paint and brushes and turpentine and overalls and marble from Carrara or wherever. No, there was just one church then worth its salt and the salt of all these artists' sweat. What church? C'mon! The Catholic, of course.

Now it's become fashionable nowadays to give the old Catholic Church a fair bit of stick. To give them a bad hiding, in fact, from time to time. And, I suppose, like any institution, it's got its faults and deserves its critics. But Florence is a city of interiors and most of them are church interiors, and that's just how it is. Okay, it's not the kind of place you go for picnics, though the Boboli Gardens were nice for the first half hour or so. Then again it's not every day you get to see so many of those tondo things, those frescos and paintings hidden away in every nook and cranny. Even the full impact of the Baptistery in the Piazza San Giovanni, whose Ghiberti doors Michelangelo himself pronounced 'worthy to be the gates of paradise', is only fully appreciated when you find yourself in its high, cool, hexagonal interior.

'Let's go,' said Flo.

'What?' I said. I was looking at these strange designs on the walls, trying to keep out of the way of Japanese tourists with video cameras, trying to soak in as much of the atmosphere as I could.

'Let's go, Fran,' she said. 'I'm bored.'

Bored? Bored! As I say, Flo is very keen on the great outdoors.

'What happened here may be beautiful, and of course it is, really,' she said, disarming as always, 'but how can you just ignore all that corruption?'

I said nothing. What could I say that I hadn't said that morning or the day before?

'And the vanity of them!' Flo went on. 'Do you think any of those artists was in a position to say, "No, I really don't care to paint Jesus again, or one of your stinking little brats, or your horse, or some saint with the eyes rolling back in his head. But what about a little dog fetching a ball for over the altar, or a child with a tear in his eye or a couple dancing?" Fran, do you really think Picasso could have flourished here?'

She was changing her weapon again.

'Or what's his name, Andre Breton?'

Breton! I thought he was a singer.

'I mean, I don't see any two-headed women playing the guitar up there, do you?'

I had to admit it, I didn't.

'But maybe, Florence, Flo,' I said tentatively when we'd stepped back outside, 'maybe this is something someone like you can't ever really understand.'

'What do you mean someone like me?'

Flo had this way, when she got angry, of looking herself up and down as if to say, I am here, amn't I? I *am* hearing this from you, amn't I? Sometimes it was cute. But sometimes, like now, it was incredibly irritating. It was as if she was saying, I'm right, so why the hell aren't you agreeing with me? And she was doing it now, pushing up her tiny chest, holding in her stomach, moving staccato-like, like a chicken down the steps through a graceful swan-cluster of young Italian girls.

'Well, what I mean is - '

Flo stopped and turned on her heels. 'What *do* you mean,' pause, 'Fran? Why can't I understand?'

The cameras in the square were all on us, our cheap sunglasses, our creased shorts and lily white legs.

'Well,' I said in a kind of whisper, kindly I thought, 'you know... After all, you are a Protestant.'

SEX

There isn't an entry on sex in the guide book but, obviously, it's on everyone's mind. Some of the women in Florence look like they could reproduce just by looking at you. Which they seldom do, of course. Look at you, that is. Instead, they have this way of looking right through you like you're not even there. That is, after they've noted the brand of your jeans. Everything from slinky cat-suits to the lightest imaginable summer dresses, dresses you can see right through to the flesh, to the nipples, to the skin. That's what they wear. That's all they wear. The designers are good, I'll give them that. A few Michelangelos and Giottos among their ranks. Even Flo, usually quite smart, looked kind of dowdy in comparison. Though she was still my girl.

Still, I did notice she didn't have much to say about the men, although she certainly spent plenty of time looking at them. Two in particular who seemed to have nothing better to do than hang around the hotel lobby, looking all cool and smarmy when I was dripping sweat.

'What do you mean, hanging around?' said Flo. 'Who? Oh, those two. I'm sure they work here.'

'Yeah,' I said, throwing a caustic eye towards the Armani

brothers. 'If you call testing mirrors work.'

So much for our dirty weekend. Actually we did have sex, once. I know Flo doesn't like the expression, but you could hardly have called it making love. For a start, I was drunk. Not intentionally, just the second bottle of wine before dinner went to my head. And Flo was half asleep. We'd walked so much that day I could feel my nylon socks burning into my feet. We got back to the hotel and showered - showers, showers, showers, I could have stayed at home and had them free in the street! - and were sitting around on the bed, looking at the walls.

That's when it happened. Or nearly happened. Or didn't happen. What can I say? Flo is usually a very sexy woman. This time however it was like one of those Punch and Judy shows I went to see one time in Brighton off-season. Walking in the rain down near the sea front, I came to this puppet show. And I stood there and watched it, only because I was there and so was it. And it was like that puppet show now all over again. Punch and Judy, Flo and Fran. Short bursts of manic energy, all the right strings being pulled, all the grimaces and thrashing you'd expect. But, as they say in the business, nobody came.

SHOPPING

You know what there's more of in Florence than anything else? Apart from art and beautiful stuck-up women with their thighs bared and these little bodices that barely cover their boobs, and guys with shades and tight arses like they're expecting to be called up for a bullfight. Cigarette lighters. There's more cigarette lighters in Florence than anywhere else in the inhabited universe. Every homeless black émigré in the universe is pedalling cigarette lighters on every street corner of Florence, or coming up to you when you're in the middle of trying to buy a postage stamp from some guy who won't even look at you when you're talking to him, and they're standing there, suddenly, out of nowhere, going *Ciao, Hello, Okay.* Ganseys full of green lighters, red lighters, see-through lighters, Firenze lighters (that's the Italian for Florence, by the way). Lighters that play happy birthday to you or have Nastassja Kinski in the nip with a massive snake wound around her, looking like something from the over-18s section of the Garden of Eden. All I can figure is it's got to be one of two things: either they're trying to start an illegal immigrant revolution and the lighters are just a cover for their presence on the streets, or Bono and the boys are due to play a gig over there in the near future and they're arming the populace for the grand finale, twenty thousand Firenze lighters swaying in the stadium darkness, *And I still haven't found what I'm looking for.* I mean it's like O'Connell Street on a cosmic scale.

Oh, and there's a lot of jewellery shops on the Ponte Vecchio, the only bridge the Germans didn't mine when they were driven out during the war. But I don't know where Flo got the idea I could afford that sort of thing. So when she started to hint that maybe I could get her something special to take home, I just held out my hand until somebody put a lighter in it. As it happened it was one with a picture of the crucifixion.

DEPARTURE

Departure should have been a relief, from the tensions at least, and the heat (the last couple of days had been hot beyond belief). But it brought with it its own difficulties.

'What do you mean you're not coming?' I said. I was already packed, had been since early the day before, in fact, and was sitting in the lobby tossing a ten-pack of red lighters with Firenze on them in yellow from hand to hand.

'I'm just not coming,' Flo said. Armani *uimhir a haon* lurked in the background. There was only one of him now. Maybe the other had been his reflection in the mirror.

Flo, too, had noticed him, and actually smiled over. Armani, of course, didn't respond, which presumably he thought made him even more impressive.

'But what about your job?'

'I'm a writer,' she said. 'My job is to write. I can write anywhere. London, Florence, the moon.'

'You type horoscopes and death notices!'

'I write about life,' she said. 'I write about the human condition.'

And that was it. More or less. That was Florence. Dejected, I took the train back to Pisa to spend the last couple of days. I sat one whole dull afternoon hoping that shaggin' tower would do a humpty dumpty. At least then I'd have something to tell the lads at work when I got home. I drank a lot that evening and tried to strike up a conversation with a waitress who pretended I wasn't there. Even when I got sick over the counter.

In the morning I was hungover and pale. With two hours to spare before the plane, I decided to take a bus out to the airport. I thought I might at least check out the competition. I needn't have bothered: the driver drove like he had a death wish, and not just for his own death but for anyone's or everyone's within a ten mile radius - the half naked young ones crossing the street, the little greaseballs weaving in and out on their mobilettes, the old pensioners out walking their ugly dogs, and me in the back of the bus, clinging onto my bags for dear life, hungover and sick as a parrot.

And then I was in the airport with about half an hour to spare lathered in sweat, ready to vomit, not really sure what had happened, what had gone wrong, when she appeared. Standing there before me, she looked like an angel fallen off the ceiling of heaven, big blobs of paint still not dry under her eyes, her blue, mascara'd eyes - Flo. White cardigan, clinging red dress, scuffed-looking black high heels.

'Fran,' she says, probably thinking I'm going to walk right past her, look right through her, sail on by, after all that's happened. Actually I'm going up to a postcard stand beside her, reaching for a card of St. Francis of Assisi receiving his stigmata from the crucified Christ, Francis kneeling down, what looks like laser beams shooting between the pair of them, hand to hand, foot to foot.

'Here,' I say, taking her hand in mine, 'a souvenir of our visit.'

I give her the card and Flo begins to cry with the cares the world's lost souls and travellers save for airports.

That postcard sits on the mantelpiece of our flat in Dublin now. It's the one thing, apart from lighters, we brought back from the home of the Renaissance to our own new life.

Geraldine Taylor

Short-listed in the 1996/97 Fish Short Story Prize

is an award-winning writer of adult non-fiction who has recently started to write fiction. She is Educational Consultant to *Ladybird Books* and also writes children's books. Geraldine is also a University Student Counsellor. There is an embarrassing amount of autobiography in *Walking the Dog on Mars*.

Walking The Dog On Mars

Geraldine Taylor

Zeppelin TV Production Company:
Proposed 30 minute item: Working title - 'Obsession.'
Research interview 17: 14 November 1996.
Female; Louise T.

I'm not ashamed. I wouldn't even call myself silly. After what I do all day it's a harmless place to put your mind. Sorry. You want me to answer the questions on this card before I begin. Am I close enough to the microphone? Is it definitely recording? OK - it's going round. Here we go then. My name is Louise - Do you need my second name? No? OK. I'm 36. I'm a fixed-term contract social worker, working with adult drug abusers. I'm not married. Yes, I'm in a long-term relationship. And my obsession is with finding the perfect red lipstick.

Now what happens? Do you want me to just talk or will you ask me questions? Thanks. Yes, it would be easier with questions. Hang on, before you start - does it matter if I'm not obsessed *now?* When I answered your advert for obsessives I *was* obsessed. I really was. But I've actually found the perfect red lipstick since I got in touch with you. It's still OK then?

What form does the obsession take? Well, starting when I was

18, I've been buying a couple of new lipsticks every week for the last sixteen years.

I should think it's about a hundred a year, give or take, so that's probably around sixteen hundred lipsticks altogether. Yes, of course it's possible. Loads of different lipsticks come out every year and there's dozens of ranges. And I'm sure I've simply forgotten and bought the same one seven or eight times over the years. There's no system involved. I'm not keeping records: I'm not that much of a nut.

Why should storage be a problem? I throw them away. Sometimes I know as I'm buying them they aren't going to work. Sometimes it's taken two or three wearings and the truth's obvious. Of course I've thrown them all away. What else can you do with the wrong lipstick? Cost? Oh, I should think three or four hundred pounds each year. Pathetic really when you think what I'd clock up if it's shoes or rings I was after.

No, it's the *time* that's the problem. I reckon it takes me a good couple of hours to choose a lipstick. I keep walking away from the counter and coming back and putting some more samples on the underside of my index finger. Did you know that the skin there's the closest colour-wise to your lips? I read it somewhere. Then I go outside in daylight and walk around holding my finger out in the sun. I like seeing how the sun brings out the shimmer in the reds. I tend to go for the glossier ones. So anyway, it's the *time,* not the cost that's inconvenient.

I'm obsessed with the names they give the reds, too, and that can be a bit awkward sometimes. It gets in the way of my concentration at work. Say there's a client is telling me about his addiction - my mind's just repeating *pearlised poppy* over and over again. I make poems out of the names. Here's one:

Defiant cherry
Drowning in scarlet
Pimpernel planet
Ruby by starlight

Pink pioneer

Opal rain

Scarlet stain

I could probably list two or three hundred names for you, right now. OK. Another time.

How else does the obsession interfere with my life? Well, to be honest, there's the agitation and the disappointment. The agitation happens the very second I've paid for the lipstick and it's in the little paper bag and the assistant's holding it out for me to take. That's when I'm *almost sure* it's the wrong choice but I'm hoping against hope that there might just be a miracle.

The disappointment? That's when I *know* it's wrong.

Sorry. I don't know exactly what started it. You *don't* know and that's something you learn in social work. It's pointless asking *exactly* when things started to go wrong. You can't be exact. I mean, how far back do you want to go? What happened when I was a kid - or what happened just before I started buying the lipsticks on a regular basis?

Yes, I can help you with that. There is a specific image I keep seeing, something that sort of drives me on. Yes, a *vision* if you like: good word. I remember being in Sally Lunn's Coffee and Bun shop in Bath. I was 18 and James and I had just started going out together. James was talking to me about something or other and I was sitting, listening, and looking around. There was another studentish couple nearly opposite us. She was talking and he was watching her. He was looking at her lips as she talked and I don't think he was in touch with what she said. He was just drinking her in. Not her words - *her.* All of a sudden, he picked up one of her hands and turned it over, palm upwards and kissed all her fingertips, one by one, really slowly. Then he nuzzled into her palm like a butterfly feeding on a flower.

No, I don't remember if she was wearing lipstick. Actually, I don't think she was but that isn't really what I'm talking about. Never mind. Anyway, that's what I think about just before I go off to buy my lipsticks.

How would I know the right lipstick? Well, I did, didn't I? In the end I found it. Do you want me to tell you about that now?

I'm sorry. I've avoided your question. Let's go back. How would I know the right one?

I think it would make me different. I'd be lighter. I'd grow my hair long and swirl it about. I'd have silk underwear. I'd wear shoes just made of little strips of silver leather. I'd work in advertising. James would buy me roses, not freesias. I'd go dancing. I'd wear pink. I'd be a pretty girl in pretty things.

I don't mind you smiling. It's OK, honestly. I know it's hard to believe - but some of these things have started to happen already. You want me to complete this sentence? *For me, obsession feels like...*Just one thing? That's hard. Give me a moment. Sometimes we do this kind of thing at work with the addicts. Here goes. For me, obsession feels like a lonely place. It feels like I could be walking the dog on Mars for all the connection I feel with other people. For the record, that's not all of it. There's beauty and it's hopeful - like there's me and some distant star with a special light only I can see. But sticking to your one sentence - it feels like it's lonely. So what made my obsession stop? How did I find the perfect red lipstick? Here it is, here's the page in the magazine. I'll read it.

Extract from *Being* magazine, October 1996:

The specialist cosmetic house Les Fleurs has joined up with BEING magazine to offer you the opportunity of a lifetime. A chance to have your ideal lipstick colour selected by a Les Fleurs consultant, using her scientific colour wheel. You will be presented with a free sample lipstick in the perfect colour for you!

So now I'll tell you about last week. I'd made an appointment and I had to sit on a little stool inside the *Les Fleurs* counter.

The Consultant told me her name was Michelle. She was about nineteen, dressed in a little black suit and trying so hard to be business-like. She held the scientific colour wheel up to my cheek and kept turning it round. Then she asked me if I'd mind if she wiped my lipstick off with a tissue and painted one of the sample colours on to see. She did this four times and kept shaking her head and looking at my lips and then back at the scientific wheel. My feet were shaking and my arms were covered in goose pimples. I wanted to make friends with Michelle. I wanted to take out my purse and give her all the money in it.

Then she gave a serious little nod and started to rummage round in a drawer full of tiny silver lipstick cases. She was ages sorting through them - I can still remember the dinky sound they made and then she said, 'This is the one,' and she opened the case and painted the colour on my lips. She brought me a hand mirror and, to be honest, at first I was disappointed. The red was much paler than I'd imagined my perfect colour would be. But Michelle was smiling and nodding and I knew it was going to be all right. The lipstick's called *Fragile Shell* and Michelle says it's absolutely perfect for my colouring. It'll bring out the best in me.

So - that's it really. It's the perfect colour and I'm not obsessed any more. Do you want to rewind the tape to see if you've got all this before I go? Will you call me back if you need me for the programme?

Extract from the unspoken thoughts of James A (4 November 1996 10.14 pm).
What the hell's going on with Louise? What's all this grinning and pouting about? Still. Happier than usual. Perhaps that dismal job's lightening up a bit. I hope they *don't* renew her bloody contract next time.

Extract from the spoken thoughts of James A (4 November 1996 10.15 pm).
Looking good, Louise. Looking good. Looking like a big, bright butterfly. No, don't fly away - you're always flying away. I'm going to trap you in my arms and keep you for ever and ever.

MEMO: 15 November 1996.
 To: Piers Longfellow: Producer Zeppelin TV.
 From: Annie L. - research assistant.
 Programme working title: Obsession.
 Maybe lose the lipstick story? Nothing remarkable there.

STORE RECORD CARD FOR CUSTOMER LOUISE TAYLOR:
 Les Fleurs perfect lipstick promotion, consultation 27. October
1996. Consultant: Michelle.

Name:	Louise Taylor.
Age:	36.
Birthday:	7th March.
Address:	28 Berkeley Road, Bristol.
Colouring:	Fair skin, brown hair, brown eyes.
Skin type:	Combination.

 Perfect Lipstick colour advised: *Fragile Shell*. Customer given
sample.
NOTE:
 Customer's actual perfect colour is *Bohemian Garnet* - out of
stock.
 Advised head office more promotional lipsticks needed a.s.a.p.

Deirdre Shanahan

Runner-up in the 1996/97 Fish Short Story Prize

A refugee from poetry, having started writing and publishing in that form. Studied Drama and English at University, going on to survive a three year stint teaching in London in order to write. Her work has been published in a number of journals in the United States and England, most recently in *New Writing 5* from 'Vintage.'

The Removal Man

Deirdre Shanahan

The curtains are down and patches of dust lie like shadows across the carpet. Now that the wardrobe is empty and shifted to one side of the alcove, it is easy to see the lighter patches of the wall where she should have painted. May puts a hand on the wall and feels the crunchy paper underneath. She feels even more hemmed in, her throat dry and trapped and her legs are achy from humping boxes around.

Leon comes downstairs having put on one of his records in his flat so that the tones of Van Morrison spill out, a lilting kind of old song she thinks she has heard before.

His bright face shows in the door.

'How are things?' he says.

'Oh, fine.' She opens her arms to the flat. 'Just don't know how I'll get out of here.'

'I can give you half a day to get you started.'

'That'll be great.'

'It'll be between jobs.'

He has the same easy way he had when he called round to size up the flat for the van. He is slightly built and she can not imagine how he will manage the boxes of materials, brocades, felts and ribbons along with dresses and records, all her junk, some of it useless, some precious.

'Where do you want to start?' she asks.

'Big rooms first. In here.'

'Not many in this place.'

'I'll get this lot down and then do the rest.'

She nods and he bends down to a tea chest with the agility of a lithe dancer and his long, thin, single plait falls down his back.

'Jane Austen. Do you want to keep her or throw her?'

'Oh, throw her. I don't even know how it got here. The girl I shared with must have left it.'

'Brainy eh?'

'Yeah, I don't know how I got to know her. She must have been desperate.'

He looks thoughtful for a moment and adds, 'You're right. It's not easy to find someone to live with.'

'No.' She paused. It was not, that was why she was moving on. Sharing had been easy but getting out was easier.

She leaves him to carry the rugs out to the van. It is only nine. He has come early, earlier than she expects and she feels caught unawares, as if half dressed. He would be seeing the shabby habits of years, stuff she should have thrown out, window sills needing painting. She hopes he will not notice, that he will not care. He does not look as if he will, with his baggy pants and light tan. When she comes back he is scouring around the floor. He picks up a fag end and slings it out the window. She wonders what it would be like to have him around. Would he always be so tidy?

'Have you always done this?' she asks.

'Only since I came off the road.'

'Oh.'

'Anyone can get into it. Well almost anyone. I had a friend in it and I needed a job when I came back. I was travelling for three years after my marriage broke up. Gave up my job at a butchers and just went off. I was lucky, being on the road for so long you don't know about jobs.'

'Where did you go? Around England?'

'Bits, and Ireland too.'

'Did you? Where?'

'The west. Donegal. Places like that. I met some really nice people there. It felt very different when I got back. Takes a while to settle, especially when you've been on your own. Is this going?' He holds up a small stool.

She says yes and then realises she is in the way.

'It's awful all this but it's my work.'

'What do you do?'

'Make hats.'

'Hats? I never met any one who made hats before.'

She tells him she went to art college and he says he met a lot of people on the road who had been to college or university.

'They had PhDs, degrees, everything, but they couldn't stick the pressures. Some of them were really clever, lent me loads to read.'

Yes, she says. She knows. Everyone has to have time out once in a while. She looks at him carrying a wicker chair out to the van, and when he comes back he says he went to a Druid wedding when he was there.

She nods. She knows the scene. It was like that years ago when she was a kid visiting, the whole place flakey with people who could not live in the system. She remembers the fields and the sky and it is as if she is not in the room but somewhere else, in the mountains with the wash of rubbly walls, sheep, small houses. She keeps looking at him. She could mention places he might know and wants to ask him but thinks not now, not yet, and she feels as if she has known him a long time but that is impossible. He has just told her he is originally from The Ridgeway, a local boy who made a long journey out of the place once and returned.

In the kitchen all the cleaning stuff still has to be packed.

'Shall I start on the drawers?' he asks.

'If you can.'

'We must remember to leave the kettle and cups,' he reminds her.

'Of course.'

He pulls at a roll of wide tape and sticks a piece over the holes of a tube of Ajax, so promptly and efficiently she thinks she could do with someone like him, as he wraps each bottle in paper and puts it in a box by the door. When it is full he carries it out to the hall to join the others. She watches and feels strangely protective. She has moved before but never has anyone helped her so much. She stands by the counter trying to do something useful, like gather the plates, wrap each in paper and lay them in the box.

'What about in here next?' he calls.

'OK.'

There it was, all her old clutter hanging around, and her hats, packed in a room as large as a box. At least moving would give her more space.

'I really liked it over there. Slow going, easy. I used to camp. It was weird, the places I got to, cottages, castles in ruins, big houses neglected way out in the country, kind of left over, at the edge of the world.'

She thinks of houses she knew there, crumbling trails of stones on the ground in a small place, a name he would never know, almost part of her imagination from a time when each day was indistinguishable from the next.

'This is nice,' he says.

'You like it?'

He nods while looking at the tall dresser heaped up with bits of paste jewellery, fat brooches, ropes of thick pearls, photographs of cousins, aunts, uncles. Her grandmother with her hair in a bun and her mother when she was twenty-one in a nice dress with lace cuffs.

'I don't know why I've kept them. They were taken a long time

ago in a village in the west. Shraheens.' She stops, not intending
to give away so much.

'They've just accumulated,' she adds.

'They're like a kind of shrine. I've got a Buddhist friend who
has something like this, sort of altar.'

'Altar? I guess it is.'

'Shraheens.' He repeats. 'I think I went there. Is there a ruined
church with a cemetery by a river?'

She says yes and wonders if he has visited it. No one ever did
unless they had to.

'Yes, I'm sure I went there.'

The moment stuns her. Not many Londoners had lived for any
time out of it. The gardens out the window are light green, the
trees at the end melt like shadows but she has to move, to step
aside to let him take out the drawers. She wants to ask him did
you by any chance run into my uncle? Did you see him in a pub
or on the mountain? Were you possibly in his house? You might
have been. It was neat and small and he was very hospitable.

'There's that statue by the church, to some priest or other.'

'I think there's something like that.'

'He helped a lot of people at the time of the famine.'

'Did he?' she asks.

'It says so. There's a plaque.'

Was there? And then she remembered, something written
along the side. So he had really been there. All that way from this
city to the village.

He stands up and a paperback stuck in his back pocket
bulges. She thinks of Uncle Jed and the way he kept things
stuffed away. Books, cigarettes, old papers, though everyone said
he had his face in the clouds and that was why he got chucked
out of university, that and the drink though he had seemed
amazing to her, the way he strode down the fields and she had
always liked his open face, ready to laugh through the days of a
long summer.

She spent time with him, gathering in the cows for milking and taking them back again. His dog yelped up ahead and he held her hand and told her names of things. There was ragwort, cow parsley, kelp, mussels and winkles. He knew so much.

'What are you thinking?' Leon asks.

'Oh, nothing.'

'About over there?'

'Actually yes,' she says and thinks how that said everything. She was here and all those things were from where she had been, in the past.

At one he finishes clearing the flat of the big furniture.

'I'm off,' he says.

'Righto.'

She looks around the empty space. He has done a great job.

'What time tomorrow?'

'About ten. I've got a load to drop off.'

'OK I'll be here. I can't go anywhere,' she adds.

He leaves with all she owns packed in boxes.

Later she hears the sound of his footsteps, a door thud and the flash of water as it runs through the pipes they share. He is hosing himself down, she thinks, for the night. He would be going out and she would have to stay here. She sits among the boxes, watching the TV that he has left out.

She lies on the sofa opened out as a bed, under the gaze of the bay window. If only things could stay the same, she thinks, if there was no moving, no having to pack up every few years. Old black and white photographs stare at her. She has not looked at them properly for years. Jed in the fields, his back against a hay-rick and his legs sticking out to the camera and she remembers the times she and her parents stayed in her grandmother's house. She must have been eight then, such a young time, so far away but she remembers clearly because of the new cooker and her parents arguing over the regulation of heat. That was how they communicated. Her mother would be cooking and her dad would

142

come up behind her.

'Have you ironed me shirt? Did you get that bit of a lamb I was telling you about?'

Her mother's pale face looking up, a faint spark, saying she had not.

Him turning the knob back.

'You boil everything. Look at you. Can't you see the spuds are nearly burned?'

Her mother, laden with thoughts, saying nothing but when he was out of sight, turning the heat up.

There was more peace when they ate, like the times when Jed was up at the house, lured by her mother's cake or bread, her thick sandwiches of cheese or chicken. She made pies where the fruit oozed lazily and she cut him pieces diligently as if Jed was an important person and not the small-time farmer of a few cows and acres they knew him to be. He captivated her with a kind of charm she had only ever glimpsed in other men, a kind not possessed by her husband.

She remembers a dish of bacon, steaming, its pink salty flesh in the centre of the table. Jed had given himself a dollop and a thick lash of fat lay on the curve of his plate. The room was dark with the only light coming from the open fire.

'A drink Jed?' her father asked, coming to the table with a clutch of bottles.

'I will so.'

Later as she sat up in her room she heard Jed belch and break into song.

'The harp that once through Tara's halls
The soul of music shed,
Now hangs as mute on Tara's walls
As if that soul were fled.'

His voice cracking and lilting around the room below until she heard the front door slam at midnight.

Early next day Leon knocks and catches her doing her teeth

but it does not matter. He smiles when she lets him in and he gets straight to work, heaving out the big boxes into the van.

'That must be nearly all the big stuff. What will you do with them?' he asks pointing to the trinkets and photographs.

'Pack them.'

'You sure you don't want me to do that? I know how. Loads of paper round each individual one, that's the trick.'

'If they got broken I'd feel awful.'

'Of course. Who's this guy? Your dad?'

She shook her head. 'My uncle.'

'He looks happy.'

'He was, mostly. But he never married.'

'Ah that explains it.'

Leon laughs, and she remembers her mother's light, cheery voice through the house saying, 'Ah, he's a grand man that Jed, when he's in form. You can get a good song out of him, sure as a cup of tea.'

'There was a good few women after him, when he was young. Him and his land. I can tell you,' her dad had said. 'I don't know why no one ever got him. He would have been a good catch. The best I'd say, him with the fields up from the sea and good drainage. I don't know why he went letting them to that son of Maguire. Soft in the head.'

He talked on regretting his own lack of land now that he had moved to town and May listened, quiet as the turf that flickered in the low fire.

'An oaf of a fella. I'd never credit that he was my brother or that there was learning in him.'

With him blathering and her mother occupied, it was easy to slip away, letting the door fall to a gentle shut and run up the road, past the neighbour with the barrels and the scrubby hedges. She would not be missed for a while, just thought to be up in her room or feeding the chickens or having gone down the fields rambling.

Leon catches her fingering the ribbons and she looks up to find his eyes on her.

'Oh these. I don't know how they got here.'

The sides of the wooden box in which they were stored glow, though she never polished it.

'Old things,' she says. 'Bits and pieces,' and she thinks how they are still there, stones from the beach, dried flowers, sheep's wool, a wallet. She has hung on to them and. she thinks of how they arrived in her life, unbidden visitors, in the way she had found herself once in Jed's house that morning and whether it was because she was too early or he was late getting up she did not know, but there was no sound from the house, no radio with the news, no thud of his big feet.

Surely he had got up. She paused and went in down to the kitchen, passing his bedroom door. Still no sound. She went on out the back and there he was, humming, totally at home with himself.

He turned to reveal a great blob of pink hanging in front of his trousers with his hand round it. His piss sprayed on the grass, a delicate arch coming out of the great bit of himself like a big sausage she had seen in Maguire's, the kind her mother said were better than the ones in packages. She went stiff with surprise.

'Sorry. Sorry,' he said as he rummaged around with his clothes, putting his thing back like he would a kitten in a bed of straw down in the barn.

'Don't be afraid. Come here a minute, I want you. The toilet was blocked, you see. I had to come out.'

He tucked in his shirt and the teeth of the zip closed. He walked ahead to the house as if nothing had happened while she followed, calmer now that he had made his explanation. It was obvious. What else could he do if he could not use the toilet?

In the kitchen he was going though a drawer in the dresser. It was packed with heaps of rubbish, her mother had always said, but he seemed to know what he wanted. She felt his

145

awkwardness as he scrabbled in the drawer, shifting things from one place to another.

'Here.' He held up a long leather purse which she recognised as a wallet. The kind men had. 'Don't say a word about it.' His pudgy face looked down at her. 'You won't breathe a word, will you?'

His face looked unusually strained and she could not tell why because she had not minded him not being in the house. She shook her head. She had known him so long. He had shown her the jennet in Patsy Fagan's field, a golden cow and a bull with one horn, so many things that she could not think why he looked worried.

'It was nothing. Just a song. We'll say it was my song you heard.'

He put the wallet in her hand.

'This'll be our secret. You see it has the two pockets and this one, you wouldn't know it was there.'

Her fingers ran along the sewn edges of large dark stitches tricking one after another.

'Twas specially made, that was. Hand done. But you can keep it. I was only after saving it for some occasion like. Something special.' He was looking at her and she felt locked in, caught, as if all he said was falling on top of her. His bulky body was close, suffocating and she looked up again to where his palm was outstretched and saw the soft dark tones of the leather.

'If you come round here now, I'll give you a wee drink.' He reached up to a cupboard and brought down a bottle like the kind her dad kept hidden from her mother, on top of the wardrobe.

'I'm going to have a drop, will you join me?'

She stared at the pretty label of gold letters and the big words and said yes because she knew she had to.

'It'll do you good, warm you up. But you mustn't go telling about this either. D'ye hear?'

She shook her head and took the glass like an egg cup,

holding the drink of a golden colour, richer and deeper than the long spray she had seen in the garden, where it splayed in a semicircle of light. The drink burned inside her and she did not like it but the dark leather wallet lay in her pocket like a jewel till she got home and put it in her case under a jumper.

She bumps into Leon as he leaves the house carrying the fine wooden box. He smiles and she feels pleased because everything is in the van.

'After this we'll be off,' he says.

'I'll be glad to get out and settled in somewhere else.'

'Have you got the key for the new place?'

'Yes.'

'See you then. Bye.'

'Bye.'

She watches him speed off in the van taking her possessions into the distance, down the road. That part is over, she thinks. The part of living here, is gone.

When she gets to the flat, he is already there.

'The previous girl let me in.'

'That's good. And you've started to unpack.' She is surprised but delighted because suddenly the prospect of all she has to do before she can feel she is living there seems such a lot.

'I've just straightened out a few things, like the ones you'll need in the short term.'

He makes a cup of tea.

'I couldn't have done this alone.'

'Don't think about it. Where do you want the stuff? Just tell me which room.'

'Here. I've made a plan.' She looks in her bag to find the paper.

'I'll start with the sofa first and then the rest.' He unscrews the doors and lays them against the walls.

'I'll have to be quick getting this lot unpacked,' she says looking at the three cardboard wardrobes which held her clothes.

'Why?'

'You want them back, don't you?' He shakes his head.

'No hurry. So many are out, it won't matter.'

'But I thought I could have them for only two days.'

'I'll say I've got a private job. They won't notice.'

'Thanks. Look, I picked these up on the way over. Have one.' She holds out a pack of ham sandwiches.

'No thanks. Bread'll do me.'

'Is that all?'

'I don't eat meat. Never touch the stuff. Ever since I went to an abattoir about the time of the break up, I went off it.'

'Oh, of course. Sorry,' she says though she can not tell why and then she thinks of his loneliness all that time ago which had set him travelling in the first place. He goes into the kitchen and is pulling the washing machine towards the wall and attaching it by the long tube to a hole. She feels a pang of loss and sadness that he had disrupted his life, trying to cut himself off from the past. She wonders if he knows where his wife is and if he has met anyone else.

'You gonna set up your business here?' he asks.

'Hope so, soon as I get organised.'

'Yeah, that's the thing, get into it quick as you can.' He sits on a box, one leg across the other and munches on a dry roll with a lavish spread of jam on top. He looks boyish and very young, as if out of another age and in seconds is up again, taking the standard lamp she had bought from a junk shop, out of the van.

'In here?' he calls.

'Yes.' She follows him back and forth as he carries small drawers and plants. He puts the trunk in its place under the big window and in moments all the big furniture is at rest. She looks at him with a mixture of gratitude and amazement that he has done so much and so soon. She shuts her eyes to think, to clear her head of all she feels, of the day and its activity and a tiredness she has not known before floods through her arms, her legs and all her fingers. She feels old, older than the seasons, as if she has moved through years. She cannot help herself but go close and finds her head sunk into his shoulder and his face turning towards her.

Their mouths fight and his arms which all day have carried her possessions back and forth hold her. He leads her out of the room to the sofa and draws her down so that she sees his sharp blue eyes even more clearly and thinks how she has seen this blue before, somewhere far back and she thinks of Jed and the wide open sea near where he farmed.

'What are you thinking of?' he asks.

'Just places. Places I've lived in.' She pauses. 'I haven't been back there for years because I thought it didn't matter, that I was just travelling through. But really, I've never left. It's still inside me. Even though I was just a summer visitor.'

She thinks how he has youth on his side and can carry her to a time when she felt safe, make her new, young again. She wants to let him loose on her because he has been through her life, carried its fragments out of the flat down the street to here. He knows each part, though he does not know and cannot, what they mean, how they intertwine, crashing with their own private resonances down and down again.

She likes his hands and the way he does things. They are pale and lean like the lip of waves, or feathers. She thinks of gulls, the crisp of foam always, always coming in.

'You can't be young forever,' he says.

'You can try.'

'You can live back there in your head but it doesn't work. I know. I've tried but sooner or later you have to let go before the past makes a mess of you.'

She listens. He is right of course. You have to forget the things that hold you back.

He raises himself, a long clean body and slides in between her.

'You have to think of now,' he says, 'right now,' and he goes deeper.

In the morning she rises alone to find that only the thin net curtains the previous girl left protected them from the gaze of the street. There is just her and her possessions. What did I expect? She thinks. What did I think would happen? She makes tea and sits in her dressing gown looking around at all he has left there. The table, the chair, the cooker. She dresses and looks out the window for his van, as if it would be there, but there is only a trail of cars and so she mooches around distractedly like a person who has lost something.

She takes her books out of the boxes and puts the plants in the light. She checks the drawers and roots around for a pair of socks and then she finds it, the wooden box with the shiny sides wrapped amongst a wodge of towels, exactly the way he must have left it, because he knew how to pack.

She opens the lid and there they are, rough stones, pink shells, old rings and her fingers go through them but no matter how much she tries, jabbing at the trail of coins and old tickets, she cannot find the wallet.

'Christ,' she breathes. What should she do? Go round to his place and demand it back? But how does she know he has taken it? How can she be sure? And so what anyway? It is a small price to pay for so much help and Jed is buried now. But she had loved that wallet as a precious thing.

She gets up from the floor and goes to the wardrobe with the small mirror inside. Taking a pill-box hat out of a box, she sets it on her head and purses her lips at herself. Moving side to side she pretends an elegance. Is that the right word for the dark blue velour hat with two small bows she has attached discretely? She wonders and feels it must be. She has made these for years. There are several versions of this design, one with a huge bow at the back, others without, some with varying amounts of net, but she prefers this one best. How did she get into this, making odd shapes for women to plant on their heads? It seems strange, not quite real, not proper work, but something she seemed always to have done and anyway she always likes the feel of small things in the palm of her hands.

She moves her head back and forth, and tilts it so that she appears grown-up and though she stands in her crumpled tee-shirt, with her hair awry and her face not done, she feels she could be.

Sheelagh Morris

Runner-up in the 1996/97 Fish Short Story Prize

Born (Dublin) late Dec.'39 - why couldn't my mother have held onto me until January, and I'd be a whole decade younger! Married 1965, now separated, two sons. I write short stories mainly for radio, (RTE / BBC). The pittance earned is not enough to keep my one-eyed cat (the only *real* character in my story; chubby friends, stop identifying with the heroine, it's not you!) in the style he prefers, so part-time lecturing provides the cod for him and the chips for me!

Letter to a Cat

Sheelagh Morris

'Colonel Blimp do you think that fascism is carried in the genes? Like cystic fibrosis or haemophilia?'

There was no answer. Norma had not expected one. She turned over the page of the Sunday supplement article on genetic engineering and looked up again with a quizzical expression on her face. Still no answer. She didn't repeat the question. Her husband, Daragh, and June, their only child, were drawing up a list of invitees to June's forthcoming wedding. The 'Colonel Blimp,' whose opinion had been sought, was a fat, one-eyed tabby cat. His usual response to her many questions, rhetorical or otherwise, was a contemptuous stare from the functioning eye.

She knew that the cat did not enjoy her conversation, but he didn't tell her to stop talking rubbish or ask what they were having for dinner. Over the past few years, and more so since last January when June had joined the family firm of accountants, father and daughter treated Norma with, on good days, condescension and, on bad days, contempt. Most of the time they ignored her.

'We don't have to ask Pat Dineen, do we, Daddee?' Norma smiled to herself at how kittenish June could become when wheedling favours. 'He's not that important a client. I'd far prefer to ask Janet Dickson and her husband. She's terrific fun.'

'Whatever you think best, June,' Daragh acquiesced, as usual, 'but we certainly must ask the Hughes. They've done business with us for donkey's years.'

Norma looked up from the paper. 'You're not forgetting your cousins in Naas, June? They asked us to all the family weddings.'

'I'm not asking them.' June's tone was stubborn. 'There's far too many of them. But I suppose we'll have to ask Aunt Mary and Uncle Tom.' She clicked her tongue with annoyance as she added their names to the list. 'They're no earthly use to us and there's lot of people who should be asked.'

Norma put down the *Sunday Tribune* and looked Colonel Blimp straight in the eye. 'Colonel, do you think it acceptable practice to ask only the useful and or decorative to your wedding?'

June swung around in her chair. 'Mother, would you stop pretending you're talking to the cat.' She turned to her father for support. 'The reception is going to cost a lot of money. We have to get some company advantage.'

Daragh suspected June was going too far but he was mesmerised by her business acumen and single-mindedness, (not to talk about the steadily growing pool of clients since January).

'Mum,' June's tone became conciliatory; 'if you want to help, why don't you go and try on your wedding outfit again? It may need altering.' She smiled sweetly as her mother left the room.

Upstairs in her sewing-room, Norma eyed the wedding garment. She had no desire to 'try it on' and the only suitable 'alteration' would be to move it from the wardrobe to the dustbin. She had let herself be coaxed by June, against her desires, into this port-wine suit, straight as a box, with small lapels and a sensible kick-pleat at the back. Worn with the accompanying wine pill-box on her head, she would look like an elderly Rumanian air-stewardess. The selling point for June may have been that the wallpaper in the Wedding Reception Room at The Glen Cross Hotel was exactly the same shade of plum/port/maroon and, with luck, her sixteen-stone mother would fade into the background. All that would appear in photographs would be a large, pale bewildered face. She shoved it impatiently to the back of the wardrobe and pulled out her own selection of desirable 'mother-of-the-bride' outfits.

Norma would have been a success in Egypt, Turkey, Iraq - countries where real women are appreciated, thighs and bellies, rolls of fat and all. She believed in emphasising reality. Over the years, as she got fatter and fatter, she had made wider kaftans of wilder and wilder hues - shocking pinks, deep ambers, sari-peach, sour apple greens, bordered with gold and silver threads. Some of the more elaborate had mirrors emblazoned on the front and dangled ropes of pearls and semiprecious gems. They were works of genius, lovingly created in the lonely hours of a misfit's time. She tumbled them onto the studio couch and gazed in admiration. She took off her dull afternoon dress and, picking up the acid green, slid its silky folds easily over her Rembrandt body. The ropes of glass and the mirrors tinkled as she moved. She was an amazing sight - an eighth wonder of the world, femininity under full sail. But, it has to be said, not suitably garbed for a suburban wedding. Nor for anything else. Norma never wore any of these creations. She had put on the crimson satin once to go to a dinner at the golf club but seeing Daragh's apoplectic expression had gone back upstairs to change into her black Jersey dress. Now she sighed and, taking the green silk off, hung it carefully back. As she did the maroon cage fell to the floor. She left it there and hastily pulled on an old tracksuit.

Coming down the stairs she could hear Daragh and June making tea and agreeing that the Dineens might be asked but under no circumstances could they bring their adult Down's Syndrome son.

'I'm going for a walk,' Norma shouted from the hall. 'There's shepherd's pie in the fridge.' She slammed the door of *number 42* behind her.

A steep hill led down to the beach. It took her about seven minutes to reach the coarse sand. It was a cool day although the sun was shining. A few children were messing at the edge, splashing water and throwing dollops of sand over their bright, clean clothes. They paid no attention as she sailed past. The wind was behind her and she moved quickly. She was feeling much better now. She took off her shoes and let the water at the edge chill her toes. Let them have their shepherd's pie alone; she wouldn't go back until dark. With a bit of luck, the two of them might have gone out to meet Francis, the intended, for one sensible nightcap. They'd sit in the local, pencils at the ready because lists and calculations must be made. Francis was of like mind and June would be happy with him. It's marvellous when birds of a feather flock. They'd run a tight ship together and, unless there was some genetic throwback to their grandmother, their kids would make the perfect crew. 'I'll visit on Sundays,' Norma thought, 'and keep my mouth shut.'

Suddenly a piercing pain went through her and she toppled over onto the wet sand. She took hold of her foot and felt the hot sticky blood flow through her fingers. She bent over to look: a deep cut was gashed through her big toe. She sat for a while wondering should she suck it to clean away the sand. But she thought perhaps not; she was on the large side for that kind of aerobic. A shadow fell across her and looking up, she saw a thin gentleman looming over her. With one smooth movement he was sitting by her side. He leaned across and picked up a sharp razor-clam shell tinged with red. 'That's what did it. Show me the damage.' Norma allowed him to take her foot in his bony hand. He drew in his breath.

'That's deep. Needs to be cleaned.' Standing up he took her hand and pulled her gently to her feet. 'Come back with me. I live up there.' He pointed to the scrub grass. 'You can wash it and dab about with TCP.'

She followed him meekly, limping slightly, her shoes in her

hand. The thought crossed her mind that he might be a pervert who liked fat women with bleeding feet. He would take her into the long grass and plunge the razor shell, which he was still carrying, deep into her fleshy white throat. She shuddered.

'Cold?' His tone was concerned.

They dipped down into a hollow in the dunes. Just ahead was a tin shack, large for a shack and brightly painted yellow. But definitely a tin shack.

'Home,' he announced with a wide smile and suddenly he was almost handsome. He was middle-aged, with mousy hair losing its grip on top, so thin that you feared bones would surface but the smile made Norma feel comfortable. He pushed open the door with his foot. It was dark inside because almost all of the windows were small and high up. On first impression it seemed to be just one large room, full of clutter and confusion. But Norma could just see a staircase leading to an open gallery; through the slats of the banisters the corner of a patchwork quilt was barely visible. That must be the master bedroom. She giggled.

The gentleman ushered her to a very large and battered armchair over which an Indian rug was slung. She sat down gratefully, her foot really aching.

'Just a second.' He vanished into the darkness of a corner and fussed about. She looked around the room. It was lined with shelves of books - hundreds and hundreds of them. She tried to read the titles but the light was gloomy and she hadn't got her glasses.

'Let's have a look.' He was back with a bowl of water, a towel and a bottle of disinfectant. He was very gentle with her foot. Norma closed her eyes and smiled; it was nice to be looked after.

'What are you smiling at?' He seemed really to want to know.

'I feel like Jesus.'

He made a gesture of despair towards his thin locks. 'I'm afraid I'll have to use a towel.'

It was lovely to find someone in your mind. It was a very long time since that had happened to Norma. He dried carefully between each toe and then put a plaster across the cut. She was relieved that she had nice feet. Fat women often have. With an affectionate pat to her ankle, he put her sandal back on and wandered back to the kitchenette, throwing a 'Lie back there and relax' over his shoulder. Norma wondered should she go. She didn't want to. She hadn't felt so spaced out in years. Her eyes had become accustomed to the gloom and she could see clearly around her. There was a kitchen in the darkest corner, with a sink and gas-ring, a dining area by the one low window that looked out on to pots of summer herbs and flowers, and a comfortable place to sit with two large chairs, in one of which Norma lolled contentedly. These excellent chairs were in front of a massive open fire-place, piled high with driftwood, already set for an evening blaze. With a shudder Norma conjured up the sterile practicality of *number 42*. By nature Norma was a sloppy housewife, tolerant of the cluttered way that inanimate objects like to live, but her husband and daughter applied the family principles of accountancy to everyday life. If an item had no useful purpose or did not, by its innate value, confer status on the owner, then out it must go. No matter that the cracked rose-patterned cup was a last remnant of a grandmother's trousseau or that the lopsided peanut dish had been painstakingly cast in papier-mâché by a favoured six-year-old friend, his small pink tongue sticking out with intensity of concentration. 'It's all useless clutter, Mother,' June had said the other day. 'I've ordered a skip. You'll be delighted when it's cleared and there's room for the wedding presents.'

In fact there was little 'useless clutter' left. Over the years, as her husband had gained his daughter as an ally, Norma had given in and allowed her home to be turned into a show house. It never looked lived-in these days. There was plenty of money to replace any item as soon as it showed dangerous signs of developing character. 'That cushion cover looks the worse for wear, June,' her father would comment. By Friday all the covers would have been replaced. All newspapers, magazines, were disposed of as they were read. Books did not furnish any room other than Norma's bolt-hole. Over the years she had taken them in for asylum along with her Singer sewing machine, her jars of seaside shells and her score of technicolour kaftans. She looked around her again. Now she could see the titles on the spines - *A History of Philosophical Ideas, Plato's Republic, The Politics of Experience, Jungian Analysis of Dreams.* She scanned the shelves for old familiars - Joyce, Yeats, or Austen, but she couldn't see any. That was the only fault in this pleasing place. There was no English Lit.

'How about a sloe gin to help recovery? I make my own.' The glass he held out to her was a Venetian goblet rimmed with gold. Very beautiful and highly unsuitable for drinking gin. She took it with delight. He sat opposite her and she noted that his glass was old Dublin Crystal with a large chip which he carefully avoided as he drank. She sniffed. There was a strong smell of rasher fat. He saw her puzzled look. 'Just making some fried bread. Sounds odd with gin but for some reason it's perfect.' Humming softly to himself he went to check on the bread sizzling sharply in the kitchen corner.

This is the life, she thought. I can't believe my luck. An enormous chair, excellent home-made gin, an attractive man (because he is attractive), the promise of fried bread. Fried bread that is never cooked in *number 42* because of the mess, the smell, the even fatter mother! Norma snuggled further in - what bliss.

Over soldiers of fried bread, they exchanged their histories. Arthur (she had expected something more exotic) had owned this hut for years. When he lived in a house with a wife called Ruth it had been a place to run to, to make his gin, cook his bread and mend his fishing tackle. One day two years ago, his wife had surprised him by running off with a very boring man with whom she played golf every Friday afternoon. Arthur sold the house, gave her most of the proceeds as compensation for the dreary life that lay ahead of her, and cycled down to live for ever in his yellow shack on the beach. With little difficulty he arranged early retirement from the college where he taught philosophy. The reduced pension was supplemented by sales of fish and dried herbs in the local market. Life became safe and simple. There had been no children to worry about and he hardly missed his wife at all.

Fortified by three sloe gins and regiments of soldiers, Norma sobbed out the story of her shrinking world. 'It's all I've left,' she whispered through another glass of gin, 'just one box-room full to the ceiling of refugees - my books, my useless shells, my fantastic kaftans.' He took her hand and they sat in their enormous chairs, he so spider thin and she so rolling large, gazing into the flames of the fire that he had lit before he poured the third gin. It was dark outside by now and the burning logs threw shadows on the walls. Norma had cast aside her sandals and her bare toes reflected the coral glow of the fire. She wriggled them in delight. She hadn't felt so happy since she was a child.

He walked her home at midnight, up the steep hill, his arm around her shoulders as she puffed and panted over the last few yards. All the lights were out downstairs. She promised to visit again the day after tomorrow and, with a light kiss on her cheek, he went bounding down the hill and lifted his long thin arm in a final salute as he turned the corner by the clump of pine trees. Norma opened the carefully closed gate and walked up the crazy paving to the house. She had, of course, forgotten a key and it was a very cranky father of the bride who finally let her in. No comment was made on her absence until, upstairs in the twin-bedded room, (carefully co-ordinated in Spring Rhapsody), Daragh, turning off the bedside lamp, said in a voice like thunder, 'Where the hell were you until this hour?'

'I met a friend and had a bite to eat,' she yawned. 'I hope the shepherd's pie was good.'

She fell asleep quickly and dreamed of June walking down the aisle in her cream silk gown, followed by orderly lines of co-ordinated wedding gifts, as specified in her computerised wedding list - fridge-freezer, microwave, bathroom-cabinet. It was a telling dream because at breakfast next morning June gave her mother instructions to empty 'her junk room' because it would be just the right place to display the presents. Anticipating opposition, she adopted her wheedling tone and promised that she'd help store everything safely in the attic and put it all back again after the honey-moon. Norma put up no opposition. Her only comment was a throwaway remark to Colonel Blimp. 'I hope you're taking this down, Colonel. I may need you as a witness.'

'Mother you're a scream,' June was in sparkling form. She patted her mother affectionately on the head as she left the room, clutching a list of prospective invitees to a pre-wedding cocktail party to be held next week in the local hotel for those who hadn't quite made it to the reception list. Mature reflection had demoted Uncle Pat and Aunt Mary to these also-rans.

The next afternoon at about four Norma strolled down to the beach and headed for the hut. Arthur was outside fiddling with his fishing nets. They walked along the water's edge and he showed her his small rowing boat anchored in the harbour. She promised to go for a picnic with him next week to Dalkey Island. By the time they got back to the yellow hut, it was getting dark. He cooked a light omelette for the two of them. No wonder he's so thin, Norma thought, he lives on nursery food; but she was too happy to care about the hollow rumbles of her tummy.

'I'm being evicted,' she said, 'me and my refugees.'

He sat up in his chair. 'Bring them to me. There's lots of room.' He gestured around the room which was chock-a-block. Then seeing her expression, he laughed. 'Well there's so much stuff, we'll hardly notice yours.'

That night in bed Norma thought about his offer. She liked the idea of her belongings being put in his care; she could take them back after the wedding. It would be easier than hauling everything up into the attic and her books would be the perfect balance to the tomes of philosophy that lined his shelves. The next afternoon she piled high the old Renault 5 with books, shells and the sewing machine. Across the roof-rack, carefully covered with plastic, she stretched out her many coloured kaftans. The battered car trundled across the scrub grass to the hut, the wind dragging free the vivid colours of the silks. Arthur stood by the door watching her with pride. An escapee from Mardi Gras, she pulled up with a flourish at his feet.

'I took you at your word.' She looked into his face for panic but saw only pleasure.

They unpacked the books and sewing machine and English Lit took its rightful place beside the thinkers on the shelves. The sewing machine was found a niche between his goldfish tank and the large ship's lantern that was waiting for a coat of lacquer and some oil. Then they embarked on unloading the kaftans. It took a long time because Arthur kept stopping to examine each in detail, mesmerised by their beauty. He emptied a sea-chest that was in the corner by the fire, throwing maps and charts and compasses into a pile on the ground and with great care and attention they laid the kaftans one upon the other and closed the lid. The most beautiful garment, the acid green with the pearls and mirrors, he kept aside and pondered where it should hang to be admired. Eventually they decided on the wall over his bed and they put up hooks and stitched fine fishing line to the edge of the sleeves. It looked magnificent when they'd finished - magnificent sails on a magnificent ship intended to carry the Queen of Sheba to a Promised Land. The reflected colours darkly glistened in the speckled mirror that hung over the fireplace.

Arthur took her hand. 'It gives a final touch. Changes this miserable cabin into a temple.' She knew he was talking rubbish but such attractive rubbish. When he led her gently to the bed beneath the majestic rigging, she made no protest. It seemed the natural thing to do. Their lovemaking took a long time with more warmth and affection than passion. Afterwards, she fell asleep in his arms. When she awoke twilight had fallen; the room was dark and she could hear Arthur singing to himself as he prepared their supper of grilled mackerel.

'That was delicious.' Norma put down her knife and fork. 'I'd be happy to eat fresh mackerel every day.'

Arthur seized the moment to ask her a question. A question that had been playing on his mind since the first time he had seen her, stranded on the beach that Sunday afternoon - the most fascinating piece of flotsam and jetsam that a roving beachcomber would tumble across in a lifetime of searching. 'Come live with me and do just that.' He took her hand and she searched his face for sincerity. She was tempted to say yes immediately to stay here in the yellow cabin and never go back to *number 42*. But caution is not so easily tossed to the wind at fifty years old.

'You're mad,' she whispered, seeing only sanity before her. 'You must be mad, but I'll think about it.'

Arthur, confident about the outcome of her thoughts, sketched out a colourful future of fish and books, of gin and soldiers, of forays to the market to sell herbs and kaftans, of long summer days and cosy winter nights adrift on a deserted sea of sand. By now her decision was a foregone conclusion. A poet can sell any future to a lonely woman. But she gave no firm answer and she left as darkness fell.

Over the next few weeks Norma spent many hours with Arthur and at times it seemed to her that the future had settled with gentle certainty in front of them but she had not said yes. In *number 42*, careful planning and scheduling meant that everything was flowing smoothly. There was really nothing much for June to do except have a facial and relax. Her father had some minor chores - polish his wedding shoes, check the size of the hired hat and persuade the hotel to provide extra champagne at cost price. Norma was, as usual, redundant. But she wished to give them one more chance.

'How do I look?' She whirled into the sitting-room at coffee time, dressed in the one remaining exiled kaftan - a Schiaparelli Shocking Pink with tiny seed pearls sewn on the bodice. It was a favourite of Norma's. She had kept it back from the cargo of goods already safe in Arthur's, not wanting to be parted from all her treasures. June and Daragh, sipping from espresso cups, did not at first look up from their newspapers. When they did their comments were curt and to the point. 'Ridiculous, I hope you're not even thinking of wearing that tomorrow!' Norma waited for a moment to give a period of grace but their noses were back in *The Times* and *Independent* and the subject was closed. As she rustled out of the room, Colonel Blimp gave her a long hard look and closed his eye.

The household would be rising early that wedding morn. But Norma was up before the others stirred and by five a.m., she was sitting at the kitchen table writing a letter. The sky was oyster pale. It would be a good day for photographs but she would not be featuring in them, not in her shining shocking pink and certainly not in her maroon camouflage. She continued to write in her broad, slanting style... 'You may miss me a little, especially at meal-times but you'll survive very well without me. Please explain to everyone, insofar as you're able, why I will not be at the wedding. I'm sure it will be a wonderful success. Yours, Norma.' Folding the writing paper she put it carefully into the matching cream envelope and, with a steady hand, addressed it to Colonel Blimp. Closing the door of *number 42* quietly behind her she headed for the beckoning shore.

THE 1997 *Fish Publishing*

SHORT STORY PRIZE

- £1,000 -

for the winner

Top 15 stories will be published in *Fish's* 1998 anthology

Adjudicators: **Germaine Greer, Eamonn Sweeney, Pat Boran.**

Conditions:
- Stories must not exceed 5,000 words. There is no minimum.
- They must be typed, one side, 1.5 spacing (min).
- Name and address should not appear on text, but on a separate sheet.
- A fee of £8 per story is required, £5.00 per story if more than one is submitted <u>in the same envelope.</u> The entry fee is £5.00 per story for full-time students and the unemployed.
- The judges' verdict is final. No correspondence will be entered into once work has been submitted.
- If receipt of entry, personal notification of results, or any other information is needed it is necessary to include a SAE. <u>Stories will not be returned.</u>
- **Closing date 30th Nov. '97.**
- Stories must not have been published previously.
- The winning stories must be available to *Fish* for inclusion in the 1998 anthology, and therefore must not have been published elsewhere prior to publication of the anthology.
- Entry will be deemed as acceptance of these conditions.
- No entry form is needed.

How to enter: Send stories to:-
Fish Short Story Prize
Durrus, Bantry, Co. Cork, Ireland.

Honorary Patrons: **Roddy Doyle, Dermot Healy.**